DEATH AT GORLACHEN

By

Barbara J. Williams

Strategic Book Group

Strategic Book Group

P.O. Box 333
Durham CT 06422

www.StrategicBookClub.com

ISBN: 978-1-60976-609-2

This story is a work of fiction. All events, characters, and location are entirely a work of the writer's imagination.

For Dwight, my husband and traveling companion

Prologue

Julia was not really terrified of Castle Gorlachen until she found the film container wedged solidly in the toe of her walking shoe. She looked back now and realized she should have said something to Inspector Walpole about it at the time, but what use was there in looking back now?

She stood rigidly in an empty upstairs hall of the castle and gazed with horror down an arrowslit at the brown bag containing the body of Professor Quayle. Two men in dark suits rumbled the cart bearing the cadaver over a cobblestone courtyard, the contents of the bag dancing and quivering over the bumps as though it were shot through with an electrical current. The grieving widow, Jeannie, walked to the side with her hand resting reverently on the bag.

Julia watched the men load the body into a black hearse. After it drove away, a uniformed police officer closed heavy wrought iron gates that clinked into place like a final exclamation mark. She shuddered to think of the once-lively talkative photographer silenced forever by someone right here at Gorlachen, but she didn't speak up about the film, and that was that.

It was burden enough that cousin Nigel's invitation to visit the castle was worded in such a way that, sight unseen, Julia instantly and unequivocally fell in love with him. Nothing could have kept her from Gorlachen. But now a racking, niggling fear seeped into her brain like spilled Burgundy on a formal English cloth. How could an innocuous roll of film implicate her in the murder of a man with whom she was hardly acquainted?

"Are you coming, Julia? We're on our way to the abbey you know," Julia's friend, Rachel, said as she came up behind her and laid a hand on her shoulder.

The unexpected voice and touch shocked Julia so completely that she swung about in a violent reaction, her purse clenched tightly to defend herself physically if need be, her eyes wide with fear.

Rachel Givens, a dark-eyed, dark-haired beauty several years older than Julia, stood before her, her face filled with concern. She wore a tan Banana Republic safari shirt and suntan slacks studded with a network of deep pockets, an outfit meant for the day's action. A sudden anger shook Julia that Rachel was so blasé about the problems they encountered at the castle, and she lashed out at her.

"Good grief, Rachel, don't you *ever* come up behind me like that again," she snarled wildly. "You're lucky I didn't smash you over the head with my purse."

Rachel stepped back and studied Julia speculatively, taking in her pink cashmere sweater and chocolate brown slacks that set off a nearly-perfect slender figure. Her long unruly blonde hair looked as though the sudden fright electrified it and ruffled it like a halo.

"What's the matter, hon?" Rachel said, a tone of regret in her voice. "You're taking this business of murder far too seriously. It has nothing at all to do with us."

Rachel sounded so sure. Julia wanted to believe her. She wanted to tell her friend about the mysterious film so they could work out a solution together, but at this point she could trust no one. And why should she upset Rachel? Julia regretted that she nearly ruined the trip for both of them as it was. She worked at dragging a quivering smile across her face.

"I'm sorry, Rachel," she said. "I wish I could take it all so lightly."

What else could she say? Would Rachel ever forgive her for behaving like a spoiled child over her cousin Nigel's lack of attention when they first arrived at the castle? Her thoughts flitted through the first two days, leaving her more puzzled than ever....

Chapter 1

"Can you believe this?" Julia ranted while she paced the floor in front of Rachel like a puma locked in a cage. "I get this warm flattering letter from Cousin Nigel to become reacquainted with him at his lousy castle, and when I arrive he treats me like I've got smallpox." They were in Julia's room in the castle's keep.

"What can I say, hon?" Rachel said in exasperation. She was getting worn out with Julia's paranoia. "I can find no way to explain what appears to be a deliberate snub on your cousin's part."

"It's infuriating and inexcusable," Julia said, her voice trembling with unshed tears. She stopped in front of Rachel's chair and tapped her toe with displeasure.

"You just don't get it, do you Rachel?"

Rachel shrugged feeling her temper begin to rise. "Okay. I don't get it. *Please* do inform me."

"I fell in love with him." Julia flinched slightly and her face held a skeptical look as though she expected Rachel to slap her.

Rachel's head jerked up. She closed the magazine she was trying to read and studied Julia.

"In love with him? That ungracious little twit? I thought you haven't seen him since you were a child."

"I haven't. I fell in love with him through the letter. Oh I know it sounds downright silly, but I can't help it. And now that I've met him I don't even *like* him. All the warm feelings are gone. *Gone.* It's such a bitter disappointment." Her hands swept dramatically through the air like a drama queen might explain away an outfit unsuited to the occasion.

"I understand what you're going through, hon," Rachel said, remorse evident in her voice. "When I was about your age I fell head over heels for our family lawyer. He was a black-eyed hot-tempered Latin who yelled at his office help and was generally rude to everyone within earshot, but he was handsome and he drove a Rolls Royce. That was all that mattered to me in those days. For a year I couldn't think of anything but being wrapped in his arms in a wildly erotic embrace."

She stopped and frowned, as though a reevaluation brought on new truths. Her mouth curled into a distasteful bow. "Now I wouldn't give that mouthy tantrum-throwing little bastard the time of day. If you find something, *anything*, you don't like about a man, Julia, forget him."

Julia sniffed and appraised Rachel as though she smelled something fetid. She chalked up Rachel's harsh remarks to a hardened woman disappointed in love too many times. Rachel was just coming out of the throes of a bitter divorce that ended an eight-year marriage after her husband ran off with a nineteen-year-old black-eyed brunette. Rachel seemed to really love the nerd, and was only now finding her way back to some sense of purpose. Still, Julia resented Rachel's self control and her attitude that she had a lock on the board of love. She had her nerve spouting such rash advice.

Julia flounced into a high-backed wing chair and shook her head in wonder that she spent all that money to fly from New York City to this Godforsaken island off the coast of Northumberland.

"Let's enjoy this trip while we can, please, Julia?" Rachel pleaded. "I don't know about you, but I'll probably never have another chance to visit a medieval castle."

Julia felt that Rachel had pretty well cut her off. She stalked across the room and pushed the heavy leaded-glass window wider, allowing a sharp damp breeze to cut through the room. She leaned over the sill to glare at the choppy North Sea. The heave and swell of a thunderous incoming tide slammed with relentless fury against the gigantic heap of rock beneath her, throwing spray fifty feet into the air, leaving a scuddy roiling froth behind. From under a sky swollen with rain, blossoming rape fields shown like polished topaz from an inlet beyond. Gulls wheeled and screamed adding their share to the turmoil.

She looked down the full length of the crudely-built castle wall. A village of gray slate-roofed houses huddled at its base at one end. "Those poor people down there probably exist to serve this castle," she said, shaking her head sadly. "It's shameless."

"You must have known something about it when you came if your father grew up here. I mean, over the years he must have given you some idea what it was like," Rachel said.

Julia recognized controlled impatience when she heard it. She knew she was complaining far more than anyone else cared to hear, but she felt... so totally rejected she found it quite impossible to stop.

"Now I think I know why my father left this place. The titled English are a bunch of stuffy, humorless, self-centered prigs." She closed the window and turned back to the chair, a frown gathering into a hard knot between her eyes.

Rachel began to laugh.

"Go ahead, laugh. Laugh your head off." Julia knew she was angry with herself more than with anyone else. The fact was she had always been afraid of the castle. Travel brochures pictured it as a savage uncivilized structure brooding sourly over the bloody history of the land. She came here from New York City only once before with her father when she was four years old to visit her grandparents. The only things she readily remembered about the trip were the things her father insisted on remembering for her.

She could still hear his delighted laughter when he recalled how she was terrified of the dark medieval atmosphere and clung to his coattail, afraid to leave his side for more than a few steps away. How, with frightened eyes and a death grip on his hand, she worked up enough courage to only peek down long dreary gray passages and inside immense cold stone-vaulted caverns at what he proudly called "one of the great fortresses that fended off the Scots."

At least cousin Nigel was thoughtful enough to assign her to her deceased grandmother's room on one of the upper levels of the keep. She gazed around her. The room was quite large with centuries-old

3

hunt-print tapestries lining the walls. A whopping full tester bed sporting turned posts swathed in a threadbare blue embroidered print anchored one wall. On the other was a regal-sized armoire with a full-length mirror covering one door. Tufted wing chairs of red velvet were placed at random throughout the room to make the space livable.

She could not begin to figure out on which level of the castle she was. When they arrived they struggled with their belongings up the twisted stone steps, wound this way and that through identical arrowslitted, stone-paved passages until she felt that without a doubt she had come through the ever-popular English maze and would find it quite impossible to retrace her steps.

A sudden disquieting shiver of unease produced a rash of purple goose bumps over her arms. She pulled her sweater closer. Once again she went to the window and leaned as far as possible over the sill, gazing timidly down the full length of the sheer rock wall into the raging dark water. She arrived at the castle just over an hour ago, and already she felt the keen distrust for the ancient fortress she felt at the age of four.

She turned from the window to find Rachel's concerned dark eyes studying her with an odd mixture of amazement and concern, but they immediately dropped back to an article in an old issue of *Majesty* magazine.

Julia studied her friend's smooth dark hair and soft blue tailored pantsuit. She was lucky to have such a patient friend. She tried to explain her behavior.

"Okay, I guess I know now what's wrong. I might as well face it. Since my parents were killed in that grinding train collision in Upstate New York two years ago I've been terribly lonely. Nigel's letter led me to believe I'd have the warmth of a family again. Obviously that's not the case."

She collapsed onto the chair and thought about her parents, about her plans to become a professional musician, and about all the jobs she held since the accident--sexy lingerie saleswoman, packing pecan candies in Christmas boxes, calculating endlessly boring insurance policies. Her parents left her a tidy sum of money from their careers on the Broadway stage. With a small portion of it she went back to New

York University last winter to finish her degree in music with emphasis on the cello.

It was the day after commencement when her cousin's letter arrived.

Chapter 2

Apprehension and puzzlement overcame Julia when she saw the name and address on the envelope. Nigel Maltby. He was her father's brother's only child, Julia's only cousin. What could he possibly want from her? In the upper left corner of the thick manila envelope was a line drawing of Castle Gorlachen, her father's birthplace. She waved the envelope in front of her nose and caught the faint scent of a masculine cologne.

With a letter opener Julia prodded here and there until the heavily glued envelope came apart and allowed a litter of papers to slide out on the desk. She picked up the handwritten letter first. The gracious flowing hand was arranged in a formal style on heavy gray stationery. Centered at the top, a gold family crest with red lions and silver-and-gold crossed swords on a rather crudely designed shield, seemed to guard the words on the page.

My Dear Cousin Julia:

I know it must seem strange to you to suddenly receive a letter from a cousin whom you have not seen since early childhood. If you remember anything at all about Castle Gorlachen from that early visit, you will understand what I mean by empty and lonely, for it is just that. My father, William Bradley Maltby, your father's only brother, died three weeks ago leaving the two of us sole heirs to the famous fortress and grounds.

I never realized what paces the property put my father through both physically and financially. Even though I grew up here, I was never fully aware of the grueling schedule required to keep the thirteenth-century buildings and grounds from deteriorating. It is of the utmost importance historically that they be preserved.

With this in mind, and as my sole surviving relative, I seek your help in determining whether the property should be placed in the care of the National Trust. On his deathbed my father suggested that I contact you for an opinion. He also expressed the desire that two pieces of our grandmother's jewelry be placed under your ownership. As you may already know, there are many lovely and unique historical pieces that are beyond mere financial value. Between us we must decide which shall be yours.

Your father often informed us of your progress in studying the cello. It would be a delight if you could manage a visit and bring music along, as the castle has a fine collection of old cellos that could use a tuning up from time to time.

One further piece of business. Enclosed is a photograph of Dunrose Manor, the country house left to your father as his share of his father's estate. It is badly in need of loving attention. Since your father's death it now belongs to you. We must determine how it is to be cared for in the future.

To help finance Castle Gorlachen, my father and I recently organized a Bed and Breakfast business. I shall continue with the plan as long as I must to keep things up.

I must confess, I long to meet you again. From your photographs at various ages sent to us by your father, I can see that the frightened fuzzy-haired child I remember so well from a former visit is now a lovely young woman. I can only hope you will find some interest in renewing our acquaintance.

I hereby invite you as my guest to join one of the five-day plans enclosed in the brochure to become reacquainted with your family history.

With fondest regards,

Nigel Maltby

Julia was immediately drawn to the warmth and sincerity of her cousin's words. The realization that her parents were first cousins passed fleetingly through her mind bringing a warm flush to her cheeks. She had not laid eyes on her first cousin for years, but at that moment, on reading his letter, she fell in love with him. Her face burned with excitement. Nothing would keep her from Gorlachen.

It came as a shock that the mighty fortress of Gorlachen, which loomed with menace in her memory, might be removed from family ownership. Maybe someday she would have children of her own and they could take her father's old tattered photograph of the castle to school for "Show and Tell," just as she did as a child. But it wouldn't be much fun if her family no longer owned it. And then, too, it would take away the fun of telling her friends in New York that the Maltby family owned a medieval castle in Northern England. Their eyes popped with fascination and disbelief. *"Cool, Julia. Where'd your family get it?"* they'd say. *"If I had a castle in England I'd go live in it. How come your family doesn't live there? Are you related to the queen?"* Julia stopped mentioning it because she didn't know quite how to respond without sounding like she wanted to brag about her family's importance, however important they might have been.

Weak-kneed she dropped down on the couch while her father's rich theatrical voice welled up from the past, reciting the family history of which he was rightfully proud. *"Once a group of eighteen fighting men went out from Gorlachen to fight the Scots, and only one soldier, a chap named Durhame, returned. It's a damned shame no one knows his name today...and there was the attack repelled with boiling oil inside the castle's barbican. The Scots were showered with it when alert guards trapped them between gates. The poor sods had no place to turn."*

The names of ancient family heroes who died defending the border country, and horrendous but heroic acts of border war, meant little to Julia at the time, but she relished her father's glorification of them, replete with pretend sword fights and the swinging of the mace.

Julia studied the photograph of Gorlachen that headed one of the brochures. The structure appeared to grow naturally out of a lumpy windswept rock as though a giant hand had reached down, found a handle, and pulled it to its full height from the rock's interior. Crude round crenelated towers manned with stone guards flanked the narrow barbican equipped with formidable toothy gates and--boiling oil?

Besides ancient collections of blue and white porcelain dishes, creamy earthenware pots, and stone-carved sculpture, the bed and breakfast brochure was filled with photographs of guest rooms adorned with fascinating period furnishings. The spiel promised a fun-filled medieval five days--a re-creation of the period's life styles and plays, the foods served, and tours of abbeys, churches, and early market towns in the area. Julia immediately consulted a travel agent.

"You'll need to make reservations well in advance, Miss Maltby," the agent said with her eyes glued to a computer screen. *"Apparently the Gorlachen package is immensely popular, nearly full already for the season."*

Julia didn't know a thing about Dunrose Manor. A tiny photograph of it, probably tucked in as an afterthought, was faded to a point of nonexistence. She pulled it closer to scrutinize it. It was no use. Even a magnifying glass didn't help. She would simply have to stand before it to see what kind of a ruin she now owned. She stared into space, puzzling over it. What was she to do with a manor house ruin in Northumberland?

Chapter 3

Julia made mechanical passes through the solo parts of Saint-Saens' Cello Concerto in A Minor while the warm vibrations from the letter bathed her in romantic longing. The trouble was that Nigel Maltby was only a name from the dimmest distant past. She could remember not one thing about him.

Julia's parents moved to New York from Northumberland to be active in the theater before she was born. She heard bits and pieces of family history when they received mail from the castle. She wondered now why she was not more curious about it, but she knew why. When a letter came it usually dealt with something unpleasant, such as an illness, or if it was a black-edged paper it announced a death in the family. She learned long ago that talk of those past days invariably made her parents unhappy so she was reluctant to ask questions.

Her father often told her a grim tale about her cousin, Nigel, who at the age of four was burned on the forearm with a branding iron in the shape of a Celtic cross. *"The iron was one of a collection of medieval branding irons that belonged to the castle from the thirteenth century,"* she could hear her father recite. *"My father, a man of extraordinary determination, sought them out and reclaimed them when he took over the castle from his father, the Earl of Northumberland."*

It seemed that Nigel and the child of friends were left unattended in the great hall. The two made a make-believe game with the irons, utilizing the fireplace which was the only source of heat for the room.

"A quite dreary but hauntingly dramatic oil painting depicting the use of the irons by medieval knights as a mark of noble protection in battle probably sparked the escapade," her father continued.

With an inner intensity pulsating like theater lights, Julia set her cello aside and ran her fingers slowly over the writing in her cousin's letter. She then read and reread the contents to try to form some mental image of the writer. Nothing enlightening came from it. Nigel, too, would have to stand before her and introduce himself.

The jewels were quite another matter. She had no knowledge of precious jewels. Besides costume jewelry and one pair of cultured pearl earrings, she owned a Black Hills gold pinky ring with a tiny diamond in the center that her parents gave her when she graduated from high school.

From inquiries at a respected jewelry store she was sent with a host of high recommendations to Rachel Givens, an experienced gemologist. Although Rachel was ten years older, she and Julia quickly became friends. Rachel tried to prepare Julia to pick out worthwhile pieces.

"Don't try to teach me about stones and such on this short notice, Rachel, there's not time. Just come with me and help me choose," Julia begged.

After careful consideration Rachel finally agreed. *"Why not Julia? Yes, I've always wanted to see England. I'll do it."*

Chapter 4

Now that they were settled in the castle there were questions to be answered from every direction.

"What were the names of those people we met while we waited at the causeway, do you remember?" Julia suddenly asked Rachel.

Rachel lay the magazine aside and rubbed her eyes as she tried to focus on a new subject.

"Well, let's see." She yawned and scratched at her ear. "There was that couple named Eldred, John and Mae, wasn't it, who said they fought in the underground in Holland during WW11? They must have been very young then. They look to be only about seventy or so now. Man, does he ever enjoy sexual repartee. In fact, he enjoys it so much you have to suspect he's impotent." She studied the toe of a white walking shoe as she thought about it. "Then there were Doctor and Mrs. Quayle from the University of Winchester...fat and forty, remember? They're writing a book about historical bed and breakfasts in Britain. He takes the photos, she writes the text. If he can capture attention, chances are he'll lecture nonstop forever on every available subject." Rachel yawned again.

Rachel's openmouthed yawns began to annoy Julia. She couldn't understand how Rachel could be sleepy. Julia was so wound up she felt she would never sleep again.

"And there was the American couple, the ones traveling abroad for the first time--Sara something or other and Jeremy Andrews," Julia added. "Did you happen to notice they were on our flight from New York?"

"Tall, handsome, with flirting brown eyes? How could I miss him? And, of course, therein lies his problem. The two are obviously lovers-- not married. I can tell by the way they touch each other. With those wandering eyes of his, she'll be a has-been before they get home," Rachel grinned.

"Maybe that's wishful thinking on your part," Julia teased, but she was also serious.

"I just unloaded one like him, thank you. Why don't *you* make a play for him, Julia? If your love life's gone sour, do something about it."

Julia squirmed under her scrutiny.

"No...no, on second thought I don't think you could handle him," Rachel decided. "You're too sweet and have been too well protected for a man like him."

It was beginning to further annoy Julia the way Rachel judged everyone at a glance. It annoyed her even more that she, herself, had never been in love. Real love. Oh, there was Johnny Marks and his noisy, smelly racing cars. Her parents strongly disapproved of his slovenly dress and his often-used f-word, so Julia gave up the relationship before anything came of it. She had never slept with a man and hated to talk intimately about it with anyone who might suspect the truth. Everyone seemed to be experienced at sex but herself. She changed the subject by fanning her hands over the room.

"Well, here we are at the castle," she said cattily. "Aren't we having fun?"

Chapter 5

The hulking presence of the castle was more encompassing than Julia imagined. The keep was enormously high with curtain walls rambling in long tentacles over the rocks like a giant octopus. There was much more of it than the head-on view of the main gate that the travel brochure touted. Julia's thoughts wandered over the activities when they first arrived.

A tall green-uniformed guard stepped from the door of a stone gatehouse directly into their path when they approached. He took their names.

"Welcome, Miss Maltby. The Master is waiting."

Julia parked her rental car where she was directed, her stomach suddenly alive with wayward flutterings. The Master? Indeed!

Abruptly, in front of them stood a well-built, worried-looking man of medium height with a cap of curly red-brown hair. Cousin Nigel? The Master? He was dressed in a stylish forest-green waxed rain jacket, tan trousers, and highly polished brown loafers. He smiled stiffly, like a mannequin, as though a case of nerves got the best of him.

In her excitement to meet her long-lost cousin, Julia forgot all about protocol. She jumped from the car and stuck out a trembling hand. "Hello," she said with a dazzling smile. "You must be Nigel Maltby. I'm your American cousin, Julia Maltby."

Irish Setter eyes that matched his hair in color swept over her.

Julia wondered while she planned the trip what her cousin's initial reaction would be to an average-height, slim American girl with fuzzy blond hair, straight nose, light freckled skin, and blue-gray eyes. Would he think she was pretty? Interesting? Colorless? When she finally faced him she was unable to tell.

The red eyes flicked over her a second time, as though to size her up for cooperation. "I'm quite pleased to meet you," he said formally, bowing slightly from the waist. Nothing in his manner said he was glad she came or that they had a lot to talk about.

The change in Julia was swift. She jumped back, retracting her arm as though corrected by an overly-severe mother. What did she expect? A great bear hug? A smile and some chatter about her trip? They weren't forthcoming. She and Rachel were led directly upstairs by one of the servants to their assigned rooms and were told to meet in the hall again at half past the hour for a tour of the castle followed by tea in the parlor.

Julia brushed her wayward hair and smoothed on glossy pink lipstick before she and Rachel strolled down the hall at four o'clock for tea. They joined and spoke briefly with the three couples they met earlier at the causeway.

A fourth couple appeared from a stairway to their right.

"Good afternoon," a casually dressed young man with slate gray eyes tending toward blue, and thick, perfectly groomed brown hair said. "I'm Paul Hampton. This is my friend, Annalisa Bowers." He smiled while his glance gathered Julia in rather completely before he looked away.

Annalisa was short and stocky with wide-set snappy black eyes. A thick black ponytail was caught with a bright green ribbon that matched her A-line dress. It snagged in unexpected places on her thick frame. "Hi," she said, and wiggled her fingers into a wave.

"Let's get on with it," John Eldred, who described himself as 'the WW11 underground man' said impatiently. Heads turned in simultaneous motion to stare at the tall gaunt man. He wore blue serge trousers with a dark blue dress shirt and a loosened red and blue flame-figured tie. Now that he had the group's attention, he jerked his plump pale wife against him with a show-offy flourish.

"We can't leave this gorgeous creature standing here all day." What might have been a pleasant, well-modulated male voice was thick with alcohol and rang with a false tone of drama as it rumbled through the hard-surfaced hall. Baggy dark eyes had a clouded glazed look. A thick tongue entangled around beaver-shaped teeth plodded a considerable distance behind what he tried to say.

His wife, Mae, cinched securely under his arm with no chance of escape stared at the floor. She had a grandmotherly look that overshadowed the tightly-fitted gray mini skirt and pink lacy blouse she wore.

"I suppose we'll have to listen to that claptrap for five days. Where's cousin Nigel?" Rachel whispered, frowning at the thought.

"I have no idea," Julia said petulantly.

"Well, that's a man for you," Rachel said. "Maybe he didn't like your looks. He didn't look all that interesting either if you ask me."

"I thought he was quite interesting," Julia said thoughtfully, peering down the hall to catch sight of her cousin. "I'm not all that familiar with my father's family, but I don't recall anyone with auburn hair and red-brown eyes. I wish I could remember something about Nigel. The funny thing is I can remember my grandmother rather well, mostly because I've seen photographs of her since. She had gray hair--she was sixty two when I came with my father--and blue-gray eyes. My father looked a lot like her.

"We came to visit because my grandfather was dying. I remember standing at the end of one of those humongous beds with a heavily-draped canopy and staring at my grandfather who was a total stranger to me. He was under a colorful pieced quilt and his eyes were tightly closed. I remember I was terribly disappointed when he didn't open them and smile at me. I thought that was what grandfathers were supposed to do. Perhaps *his* eyes were red-brown." She thought it over carefully. "However, I doubt it. I recall my father saying one time that his whole family had blue-gray eyes just like mine."

Suddenly Julia was surprised that a scattering of long-forgotten details from that long-ago trip were beginning to surface.

"Maybe the man who first greeted us isn't your cousin," Rachel said. "Did you ask him?"

"Oh, come on. He wouldn't lead me on that way. 'The *master* is waiting,' the gateman said and motioned me over to Nigel. When I took his hand I called him Nigel. I made it perfectly obvious that's who I took him for."

"May I have your attention please." A frail elderly man with a booming voice that thundered through the echoing hall stared resentfully at Julia and Rachel.

Julia stood up straighter and tried to concentrate on what he was saying.

"...establish several house rules," he continued. "Absolutely no flash bulbs are allowed inside the building. And, because of the nature of your planned weekend in an ancient castle, mobile phones are not allowed. Because of the castle's age and historical importance, it is strictly prohibited for any guest to venture alone into the roped-off areas. The rooms downstairs are not electrically lighted at night and are open to the public during the day with appointed guides only. Should you need service from the kitchen or any other type of service from below stairs, the bell rope in your room is in working order. At the end of the east landing you will find stairs to the garden which you may use at any hour. There will be a guard on duty at all times near the outside gate. We ask your cooperation as he checks luggage or any other parcels that leave the buildings. Now let us turn our attention to the history of the castle....

"The oldest parts of the Norman castle date from the thirteenth century. Today it is mainly a fourteenth-century reconstruction with later alterations that mark the change from medieval fortress to great house. However, at the turn of the last century...."

By the time the early part of the historical lecture ended and the group was well on its way down the staircase, Julia wanted ever so much to leave them and visit with Nigel, but she remembered the stern reprimand about not moving about the lower floors unattended. Besides, she had no idea where he was.

The tour seemed to carry on endlessly, one room leading into another, the guide rattling off historical facts in a repetitive way, like a talking parrot. A fourteenth-century chair here, a sixteenth-century ship model there, a portrait gallery of murky brown ancestors painted by men with long unpronounceable Italian names, numerous parlors, an immense paneled library with a frieze of ancient philosophers, and furniture built by Thomas Chippendale--on and on. She was unable to digest it all.

Abruptly her attention was caught by a cello placed upright in a wooden cradle at the end of a short hall where other hallways joined it nearby. Pale honey-toned wood was polished to a high luster. A rope cut off the hall so she could not get close enough to inspect the instrument, but she could see it was of fine quality with a bow at its side. Was it one of the collection that "could use a tuning up from time to time?"

After a thoroughly disorienting maze of passages, a great hall some seventy feet long opened before them. It was filled with colorful ancient heraldry and a magnificent collection of shining armor, like a medieval battleground. Resplendent mannequin knights posed proudly on white horses bedecked with medieval finery. The chattering group was awed to complete silence. Then they were moving on to other niches and grand halls.

Abruptly Julia found herself nailed to the floor. On the wall in a gloomy humungous hall was a monumental gray marble fireplace that had not been used for some time for it was festooned with gray dust webs. Near it on the wall was a collection of fierce-looking branding irons hanging from thin metal handles. Over the branding irons a dark painting that badly needed cleaning showed a man in sackcloth crouched in a businesslike way before a fire heating one of the irons. A very young man with a frightened wary expression peered cautiously over his shoulder. A rope along the dais kept Julia from getting close enough to the irons to make any sense of their shapes. It was terribly frustrating. Everything she wanted to see was off limits.

"Question, please?" Julia wanted to ask the guide about the irons and the painting. She tried three times to break in, but he was too caught up in his historical grinding monologue to pay any heed to her efforts to get his attention.

They passed through a Victorian parlor scaled down to livable size. Red and blue flowers danced over fabric "specifically designed for the room by William Morris." On an ornate Louis XIV desk was a scattering of family photographs. Julia recognized her grandmother and a snapshot of her father as a young man. There was a small wedding picture of her parents in an ornate gold frame. The others were unknown faces that bore a Maltby resemblance. She didn't see the face of her cousin, Nigel.

She turned to study the room and wondered how many times her father had whiled away an evening here with his family.

Chapter 6

The guide's monotonous voice caught her attention again. "...
while the state apartments are in the west wing of the castle
overlooking the garden and are off-limits to the public. Now,
let us turn our attention to the outstanding collection of copper in the
kitchen. A house was judged by its cooking...."

The sightseers, overflowing with historical facts they would soon
forget, trudged faithfully behind him down airless dark stone steps. On
a closed door leading from the hall Julia noticed an inauspicious wooden
sign, "Strictly Private." She wondered if it was the kitchen entrance to
the family apartments. She dawdled near the door, studying a collection
of wildlife etchings on the wall while the other guests moved on. When
the guide was out of sight at the bottom of the stairs, she reached out and
grasped the door handle.

The door opened onto a wide hall some thirty feet long. Waist-high
mahogany shelves along the walls held varying sizes of blue-and-white
Chinese ginger jars. On the floor was a red-and-blue oriental runner. A
Tudor linen-fold paneled door stood like a silent impenetrable foe at the
other end.

Before Julia knew what happened, the door banged open and Nigel
and a uniformed guard stood before her. When Nigel saw who it was he
stopped so suddenly the rug nearly skated from under him.

"What in bloody hell are you doing in here?" he sputtered sternly,
the red-brown eyes snapping with fury. "Don't you know these quarters

have surveillance equipment against intruders?"

"I'm not an intruder, as you so rudely put it, although I'm being treated like one. This is my father's childhood home. His family still lives here, and I highly resent being treated like a foreigner. If you don't want me here, why did you invite me in the first place?" Angry tears stung her eyes.

He abruptly stepped back, his face filled with uncertainty. Then his features softened.

"Look, Julia, I'm sorry. There is such a jumble of things gone wrong that I haven't had a chance to give you a proper welcome. If you'll do me the favor of continuing on the tour with the other guests I'll try to meet with you before dinner."

"What keeps you so busy, other than being rude to your guests?" Julia sneered. If she were closer to him she might have kicked him. She whirled around angrily and marched from the room. She intended to find a way to teach this rude little snob a lesson.

She quickly swished down the hall and into the kitchen where the other guests peered into a black openmouthed medieval wall oven. Julia was able to edge into the huddle behind the guide without being seen. She was dismayed to note that Paul Hampton's eyes were on her. They held a look of disapproval. She edged to the opposite side of the group to avoid him. What business was it of his what she did?

The kitchen was the end of the line. The tour broke up and the guests were steered upstairs and into the front parlor for tea.

"Perk up, Julia. You look like you've lost your last friend." Rachel appeared beside her.

"I happen to be a member of this family," Julia stubbornly snorted. "I don't like the way I'm being treated, but I haven't quite decided what I'm going to do about it. I think I might pack up and leave tomorrow."

"We can't just leave," Rachel said in dismay. "I've paid two hundred and twenty pounds a night to stay here, and I intend to see everything that's coming to me. Now I'm sorry if you're having trouble dealing with your cousin, but I came on a badly needed vacation to enjoy myself and I intend to do just that."

21

The two women stood in front of Julia's bedroom door and glared at each other. Julia saw from the look of determination flashing in Rachel's dark eyes that she was going to stay at Gorlachen the full time no matter what.

"Okay, you're right, Rachel," she said with a sigh. "I'd might as well cool down and enjoy what I can of it, but it jolly well burns me up."

"Yes, I know, honey. You've said so several times already."

When Julia first met Rachel she was attracted to her modest sense of personal responsibility and purpose. She was a rock-solid person who trusted her own ability to make decisions--so different from Julia's parents and their giddy friends who were never quite able to take their lives seriously enough to think beyond their show-time popularity at the moment. Julia smiled timidly at Rachel. She did not want to lose her friendship.

"You win." She shrugged and looked off through the passageway. "I guess I'll have to learn about Gorlachen from tour guides."

"Oh, I know you. You don't give up that easily, Julia. Now what are you planning?" Rachel narrowed suspicious dark eyes on her.

"I don't know yet, but I think I'm going to have to do something to get cousin Nigel's attention. You can act like you don't know me if you prefer." Julia turned from Rachel, went into her room, and closed the door.

She skipped tea and waited expectantly by the window for Nigel's visit and perhaps an escort to dinner. When he didn't show up, she and Rachel joined the American couple in the hall and walked with them down the long staircase to the dining room.

"Isn't this a blast?" said Sara Danes, the tall dark-eyed beauty from New York City. She had taken a great deal of care with her appearance. She wore a rose-print chiffon dress with billowing sleeves and rhinestone-trimmed backless evening slides that would make any woman envious. "And did you see the garden? I have never seen so many dazzling rhododendrons in one place in my entire life. These people know how to live."

Jeremy Andrews smiled fondly at her and tucked her arm through his, while over her head bright brown interested eyes swept over Rachel.

Out of the corner of her eye, Julia caught Rachel's smile in return. She may have just unloaded a man like him, but Rachel was clearly ready for a new adventure. Poor Sara. Rachel was not the type to give up easily either once she made up her mind.

"The literature claims the dining room is one of the most beautiful in all of England," Jeremy said, returning his attention to Sara. "Maybe the best of the castle is yet to come."

Once again Julia felt like an outsider. For one thing, she could see she was not dressed properly for the evening in her plain black wool skirt and matching turtleneck sweater. Black afternoon pumps didn't help the situation either. Her brain was simply too busy with Cousin Nigel's attitude to worry about how she looked. She was sorry she didn't taken the time to change into her lavender silk dress with the beaded bodice and her lavender suede platform shoes that made her seem taller and slimmer. It was too late now. She was dressed in a style and color that suited her mood. Was that allowed in Nigel Maltby's snooty castle? She turned to Rachel.

"We haven't seen the dining room, have we?" She felt silly asking, but she was so preoccupied on the tour that she scarcely concentrated on anything save her own bitter disappointment.

"No, we haven't seen the dining room," Rachel said wearily, giving Julia a hopeless look. "The guide said we wouldn't see it 'til dinner. Weren't you there?"

"Only part of the time," Julia grinned. Her breath caught sharply in her throat when she stepped inside the room.

A stone-vaulted thirty-foot-high roof and stunning blue-and-red Gothic stained glass windows revealed a grace so beautiful it was almost beyond bearing. Rugged wrought iron chandeliers hung from heavy black chains, their flickering tallow candles throwing eerie, long, dancing shadows on irregular stone walls opposite the fireplace. The fire washed pulsating waves of golden light over a heavy Chippendale table laden with twinkling silver, rose-patterned china, and cut crystal.

Why had her father never told her about this room? Had he been so familiar with it that it was nothing more to him than daily routine?

"Beautiful, isn't it?" guest Paul Hampton said, coming from behind her and thrusting a cut-glass goblet of ruby wine into her hand.

Julia jumped. Was he going to ridicule her for misbehaving on the tour? She smiled awkwardly as guilt overcame her. They stood side by side and surveyed the priceless structure. An unexpected lump appeared in her throat when she tried to express herself, nearly cutting off her voice.

"My father was raised in this castle. He moved to New York City before I was born. I heard many tales about its ancient heroes who fended off the Scots, but he never once mentioned this breathtaking room. I suppose he was so used to it he didn't think of it as anything special."

"How in the world could he overlook it? The most insensitive individual would have a hard time forgetting it," Hampton said. He spoke softly with speech habits that reminded her so much of her father that it invited confidentiality.

A wave of heat pulsated through Julia's body. She hoped he didn't think she was bragging about her father, or making him sound insensitive on purpose. In spite of his cultured English speech, no one ever quite believed it when she told them her father was raised in one of the largest and oldest castles in northern England.

She lowered her eyes under Hampton's direct gaze. Where was his friend, Annalisa? Julia spotted her across the room, her short stocky body planted firmly in front of the fireplace where she talked animatedly with Cousin Nigel.

Julia could not say she was sorry to have a quiet moment with Paul Hampton. She liked him. He certainly had more going for him than her cousin did. "Not everything here is quite medieval though, is it?" Julia said, motioning toward the table. She wanted to continue the conversation. "Forks didn't come into use until Henry the Eighth."

"Maybe the staff figured no one would notice," Hampton said, looking very sober, then smiling. "I suppose none of us would care to gnaw on leg bones and eat vegetables with our fingers, would we?"

"I know. I was only quoting my father." She laughed at his serious bent. "He always compared late discoveries or late arrivals with the fact that, 'ahftah all, the fohk didn't come in 'til Henry the Eighth,'" They laughed together and moved with the others to the dining table to be seated.

The setting and table service were so elegantly appointed that the guests moved cautiously and watched each other timidly for signs of how to proceed.

Julia didn't know any more about it than the others, but she had no intention of being buffaloed by cousin Nigel and his haughty ways. She expected to be seated at his right so they could visit during the meal, but to her surprise she was seated as the hostess at the far end of the long walnut table. He was finally going to acknowledge her as a Maltby, but he seemed to be going out of his way to make sure he kept her at arm's length.

John Eldred was on her left with his wife, Mae, seated down the table from him on Julia's right. Then came Doctor Darcy and Jeannie Quayle, Paul Hampton and Annalisa Bowers, then Sara Danes and Jeremy Andrews.

Rachel smiled smugly at Julia from Nigel's right. Julia felt her face flush with jealous fury as she watched the two of them bent near each other in intense conversation. Not only had Rachel captured Jeremy Andrews's attention, she was now working on Nigel. Perspiration trickled uncomfortably down Julia's side and splotched her sweater with a dark round stain.

"I hope we're having shomething I can eat. Heartburn, you know," John Eldred said, burping heartily while he patted his chest, then giving Mae a quivering, besotted smile. The sight of her seemed to swell his vocal apparatus. He grabbed his goblet and thrust it into the air, sloshing red wine over the silky tablecloth. "There be none of beauty's daughters/ With a magic like thee; And like music on the waters/ Is thy sweet voice to me..." To Wordsworth and that gorgeoush woman who's been the apple of my eye for...how many yearsh?" He peered drunkenly at Mae for help, but she only shrugged.

"Byron," Paul Hampton corrected. "The poem was Byron's." He reached out and guided the wine goblet back to the table.

"What? Oh yesh, Byron. I never can keep those poets shtraight. You know, you're really quite good," he said, trying to focus on Hampton. "It's usually my beautiful wife who corrects me. But, of course, one can alsho admire all these young beauties running about. What a pity a

25

married man can't get his handsh on them. For instance, that one over there with the black eyesh. Who does she belong to?" His attention was focused on Annalisa who glared at him through a deep frown.

Mae solemnly studied her hands while her husband rambled on, then looked up and smiled shyly when she felt the others' eyes on her. Shadows from creamy overhead candlelight emphasized a slightly bristly mustache that gave her startlingly white face a male look.

Julia felt sorry for Mae when she saw her quickly drop her eyes to a bowl of lettuce soup a servant placed before her. Men who insisted on embarrassing their wives in front of others were intolerable bores. Julia wondered what kept Mae from braining the hapless clod.

Suddenly a blinding flashbulb went off in their faces, pulling everyone's attention to the head of the table. Professor Quayle, a stubby round man with twinkling Santa Claus eyes and red sandpaper skin, balanced clumsily on thick haunches to include all the guests in a photograph.

"Splendid." He beamed with pleasure at the group's cooperation. "Just one more." He walked around the table to Mae and moved her chair in, taking her by the shoulders to change the angle of her body.

John Eldred jumped from his chair like he had been struck with a rock. "The lout's making pashesh at my wife," he said thickly, "and right here in my face, as it were."

Quayle's mouth fell open. "Now see here, old boy, I'm only trying to include everyone in a photograph for the book."

"The very idea," Jeannie Quayle said as her fair skin blanched with anger. "This man is drunk, Darcy. Disgusting."

John looked them all over accusingly, frowned at Mae as though she somehow was conspiring against him, then shook Paul Hampton's arm away as he tried to guide him into his chair.

"That was horrid, John," Mae said, too angry to care whether the others heard. "You're drunk as a lord again. You certainly don't need any more wine." She moved the decanter from his reach.

"But, my darling, I don't feel a thing."

The banter appeared to be ongoing with them. Julia was annoyed that the guests behaved so badly. Even though she had never been a vital part of life at Gorlachen, she found herself frustrated over the dissension. Everyone seemed to be antagonistic. She wanted the Eldreds to keep their silly bickering and cooing to themselves so others could enjoy the magnificence of the occasion. As it turned out, there was more bickering to come.

"What's with the flash?" Jeremy Andrews asked Quayle. "The literature specifically stated no flash photos. Gee, if I'd known I could use it, I'd have brought my other camera for indoor shots. By the way, if you're including photos in a book why aren't you using digital? It's so much easier and less expensive to use for a lot of photos."

Quayle smiled and considered the question. "I guess you might call me a purist," he said. "I have a state-of-the-art darkroom and I prefer the color and depth of the film camera."

"You're right to question the flash, Mr. Andrews," Cousin Nigel said from the head of the table, his voice slightly grating. "However, I have made an exception for Professor Quayle since he is including Gorlachen in his new travel book. I hope you'll forgive me. Professional photographs of the main rooms of the castle are for sale in the gift shop at the east end of the garden."

"Well, I guess that settles it," Jeremy said to Rachel, his dark lively eyes clouded with injustice. "What the hell. I don't want professional photographs, I want to take my own."

"It's a shame, isn't it?" Rachel smiled into his dark eyes and grappled for a reason to continue the conversation. "We've all paid the same amount. One would think we could all enjoy the same privileges. What kind of camera do you have?" Her attempt to keep his attention was lost, however, caught up again by the guest, Paul Hampton.

"You'll find that most of the large houses don't allow flashbulb cameras, Mr. Andrews. Over time the light has a deteriorating effect on ancient paintings and fabrics. With all of the tourism on the islands today I'm sure you can understand the problem." An arresting quality of authority in his polite voice seemed to put the issue to rest.

Julia found herself comforted by the sensible young man. She was thinking about Rachel telling her to go for Jeremy Andrews. Instantly she discarded the idea. Andrews was not her type. She far and away

27

preferred Paul Hampton. She glanced at the thick-bodied Annalisa Bowers. What did he see in her?

In deference to the disagreement, Professor Quayle put his camera aside and sat down to his soup while informing the group he had recently finished a book on the history of English food. He launched into a long dissertation on the origins of the evening's menu which was listed in order of presentation on gold-trimmed white placards at each place setting. Julia grudgingly admitted Rachel was right about him.

She was in no mood to listen to an unsought lecture. She studied the captivating room and its centuries-old furnishings-- imported blue-and-white Chinese ginger jars, fourteenth-century hand-carved figures on the mantel, a silver wine cooler dancing with nude maidens, and a rather crudely carved stone coat of arms reaching from the mantel to the roof high above them, seeming to pull from all corners the ancient lineage of the Maltby family.

For the second time since her arrival Julia was engulfed by a profound sense of loneliness at the loss of her parents. This lovely room was a part of their early lives. She was amazed that they left it behind to live as giddy modern Americans, as though they had totally blanked their rich English heritage from their memories.

"What is your line of work, Mr. Hampton?" Jeremy asked.

"Architectural preservation. I research historical sites and do what I can to see that they're preserved for posterity. There are still magnificent vaulted stone-and-brick edifices, some built as early as the eleventh century, that stand like decayed relics throughout the British Isles. They need attention right away if they're to be saved. Gorlachen is one of the places I've been studying."

"It seems to be well documented with facts and figures in the travel manuals already," Jeremy Andrews said, giving Quayle a glance of disapproval.

"Oh, but there's always more to learn about a historic building like this," Hampton said energetically. "As a matter of fact I have been looking into some of Gorlachen's historical oddities. For instance, the Maltby coat of arms over the fireplace. Would you believe it was very crudely carved on purpose to fool the enemy into thinking he was dealing with the basest kind of uneducated individuals? It would be akin to a warning sign promising violence to any individual who trespassed. If all the words were misspelled and running off the page, the trespasser might fear that the owners would bludgeon him first and ask questions later." Hampton lifted his arm to point out particulars. "Now consider the irregularity of the outline...."

Julia's eyes were riveted to his muscular forearm. Where his sleeve fell away she spied the perfectly-formed scar of a Celtic cross.

She sprang to her feet like she had been jerked by a puppet string, her chair scraping harshly on the stone floor. She grasped the edge of the table and held on tightly, pulling the cloth into a wadded knot beneath her plate.

She stared at Paul Hampton, the man who was supposed to be an architectural historian. Then she shifted her troubled gaze to the man at the head of the table who was supposed to be her cousin, Nigel Maltby. What an intolerable phony. She appeared to be near collapse.

Fake cousin Nigel leaped from his chair and bounded around the table. "Oh, I say, is everything all right, my dear? You look like you've seen a ghost." He took her arm and helped her into her chair.

Julia gazed into his rust-colored eyes, her skin burning from her discovery. Then she looked down at his arm. She wanted desperately to raise his sleeve to examine his arm for a scar, but now she was quite sure she wouldn't find one.

"I'm all right. It's...it's nothing. Something startled me. I don't quite know what it was." She sat down, confused even further when she saw him give Paul Hampton a questioning look. She unconsciously arranged her skirt around her legs.

The guests gaped from the edges of their seats.

"Nothing to be concerned about," the false Nigel said, his molten eyes veiled with concern. "Old Gorlachen has that effect on folks. I guarantee the castle is perfectly harmless." He received a slight nod of approval from Paul Hampton.

The group visibly relaxed, but their joking and laughter were mixed with tense anxiety. The episode was exactly the reason why they came to visit Gorlachen. They wanted to see and hear thrilling intimations of medieval ghosts and their attendant horrors with the full knowledge nothing horrible was about to happen to them.

"Shplendid, luv." John Eldred smiled indulgently as he lisped at Julia. "You're jush the type to get things on the move and make thish a perfect medieval experience. You'll keep thesh beauties feeling giddy about the place and drive them shtraight into our arms." He winked and patted her knee. Julia pushed his hand away. His leg worked its way closer and pressed hers. She moved, but his leg followed and his hand sought her knee again.

She picked up her fork and considered jabbing him, but her attention was caught by "Cousin Nigel" at the head of the table. She furtively studied him only to discover he was covertly studying her. Their eyes met time and again, weighing, evaluating, only to quickly dart away in another direction. She had not touched a mountainous cherry tart piled high with lavish ringlets of whipped cream and thick chocolate shavings placed before her.

"By gar, if this isn't the besht bloody meal I've had in years," John Eldred said, carefully licking excess whipped cream from his fingers. "If they ate like this during the medieval years, I can't imagine why anyone would change it." He eyed Julia's untouched dessert. "Oh, I say, if you're not going to eat that...."

"Here, take it," Julia snapped as she dumped it in front of him. At this point her anger was beginning to boil. She'd do anything to be rid of him.

Through the rest of the meal, the guest, Paul Hampton, continued to captivate the group with his vast knowledge of Gorlachen.

"...and I can assure you, this is one of the most interesting castles in all of Europe," he finished.

Julia became so engrossed in the scar that seemed to wink at her from beneath his coat sleeve, that Rachel had to actually take her by the shoulders and shake her to get her attention.

"Hello-ooo. Are you there, Julia?" she carped irritably.

In her preoccupation with her new discovery, Julia didn't realize the others had finished dessert and had risen from the table. She jumped up too quickly at the sound of Rachel's voice, spilling what was left of her glass of water, and tried to pull herself back to the gaiety of the group.

"I'm coming. Sorry about the sudden lapse." She didn't want to confide in anyone about the scar. She only wanted to get upstairs where she could sort things out in the privacy of her room.

It was nearly nine o'clock. After a hectic day of traveling and settling in, the guests were tired and looked forward to a good night's sleep. Julia and Rachel trudged wearily up the stone steps together.

A frown line gathered between Rachel's eyes. "Some week this is going to be if every little thing scares the wits out of you. What happened back there?"

"I have no idea. It must have been my imagination working overtime. Isn't that what we're here for?"

"Well, yes, but...." Rachel stopped at Julia's door. It became obvious that Julia had no intention of inviting her in for a late chat. "I wish you'd tell me what frightened you. At least we could both revel in it."

Julia laughed, somehow enjoying Rachel's annoyance. "To tell you the truth, I don't know what it was. Suddenly I felt a shock of some sort probably due to the medieval surroundings. Must I explain it?"

"Okay, okay," Rachel said. "The least you can do is come with me to see my room." She took Julia's arm and they strolled down the dark passage. Rachel's room was a corridor over from Julia's and faced the inner courtyard.

The heavy oversized oak doors were all alike and led into gigantic high-roofed, bare-floored echoing rooms. Each consisted of a sitting area with heavy antique furnishings, plus a bedroom area with a monumental tester bed. A long armoire with high narrow mirrored doors divided the two.

Rachel giggled as they gazed at the ornate bed with its moth-eaten dark blue velvet fabric twisted into bulky layers around the turned posts. "This is what's referred to as shabby elegance," she laughed. "When I first laid eyes on that bed, honest to God, hon, I thought of James Thurber's *The Night the Bed Fell.* I said to myself, 'Rachel, darlin', if this baby falls, it's bye-bye blackbird.'"

Julia had lost her taste for jokes. The room was frigid. She thought the stone fireplace looked depressingly small for heating such a vast area. It held little hope for heating the cold primitive bathroom that more than likely only hinted at an occasional basin of warm water. With a brief touch of satisfaction she was pleased that her grandmother's suite was gayer than Rachel's room, and with more colorful furnishings. However, it was just as cold. It seemed that everything about Gorlachen was cold.

Chapter 7

When Julia finally got away from Rachel's nonstop chatter she entered her room, closed the door, and sagged tiredly against it. Was Nigel trying to play some kind of weird joke on her? She began to pace the floor, examining the idea carefully. Were medieval landowners practical jokers? Was it part of the five-day package?

Her father, in spite of his wit and often nonsensical gaiety, had not been cruel. Somehow the man she now knew to be her cousin did not seem like a person who would be deliberately cruel either. What was his purpose in setting up another man to stand in for himself?

The scar of the Celtic cross stood out vividly in her mind. It was about three-quarters of an inch across and at least two inches long with a perfect circle at the crossing. The clear pattern of raised puckered tissue had to have come from a third-degree burn. Would two people have that identical scar?

Suddenly it became perfectly clear to her what she must do. She must find the great hall and examine the irons for a Celtic cross that matched the scar on Paul Hampton's arm.

She changed quickly from black pumps to soft-soled flat shoes and rummaged through her carryon for a flashlight. Thank heaven she had remembered to bring it along. Then she went into the hall, quietly closing the bedroom door behind her. Fortunately there was no one about to question her. She had no idea how she would explain herself if she were discovered prowling on her own.

A blanket of penetrating woolly darkness enshrouded the corridor. From the smell and feel of it she was convinced it was the original damp cold that had permeated the place over seven hundred years ago. Like original sin, it had been there from the beginning and would remain no matter what anyone tried to do about it. Shield-shaped lanterns hung from the roof every few feet with thick white tallow candles flickering forlornly in their centers. They gave off a slightly sickening oily odor.

Julia kept her flashlight trained on the uneven stone floor, intent on her mission. She scurried around an interminable number of passages looking for the stairs she and Rachel had gone down to reach the dining room earlier in the evening. She stopped where passages crossed and gazed to one side, then the other, in wonder. They were all alike, roughly hewn gray tunnels of stone. She must have turned the wrong direction when she left her room. Would she ever find her way back?

Her heart pounded in her ears. She could not decide whether she was afraid of the dark castle, or if she was deliciously savoring the challenge of her own furtive behavior. She smiled to herself. What would cousin Nigel think if he knew she were disobeying his orders with such deliberate abandon? He wasn't going to make a fool of her and get away with it.

At last the long halls culminated in a series of steep staircases dropping off in different directions. She hoped one of them would finally lead her to the great hall. On her left was the cello she spotted earlier in the day. She closed her eyes and tried to remember which direction the tour was moving when she first noticed it. She was totally confused so she opted for the stairs closest to it.

The staircase was narrow with two candlelit lanterns sputtering over primitive stone steps that were not all the same height or depth. She carefully picked her way over the uneven surfaces. The candles' elusive light disappeared well before she entered a lower hall. She turned on the flashlight and circled it over the area. A sign on one door read "kitchen." She avoided it and entered a high-domed hall engulfed in such vast black silence that it seemed to find an intruder unwelcome as it continued to steep in its dark treacherous history. Snarling stone lions, Maltby lions that her father had often drawn to head his stationery, guarded the entrance on either side. She could not recall having seen them before dinner.

The room was so quiet Julia thought her flashlight beam made a light tinking sound as it splayed across the floor to light her way. Could a light beam make a sound? Perhaps it was the cover that held the batteries in place. The sound so unnerved her that she placed her free hand tightly over the cover to stop it, but the metallic tinks came again. An unexpected shiver raised prickles over her body. She turned sharply, expecting to find someone behind her. Black plush was her only companion.

She directed the beam of light over jagged stone walls. Austere dark family portraits in heavy gilded frames hung in a long row on one side. On the opposite wall was a heavy mahogany fireplace that looked as though it had not seen a fire in centuries. Dust webs hung in heavy colorless wreaths from the grate. A spider web draped itself across her face. It clung to her eyelashes in a sticky glob. She mopped her face with a handkerchief then examined the walls on both sides of the mantel. There were no branding irons. Obviously she was in the wrong hall.

She moved through an ancient dining hall of some sort. She pulled her sweater closer against the cold and inched through the first door she came to. She was completely turned around. Somewhere in this sprawling catacomb she saw a monstrously large fireplace with a collection of branding irons hanging on the wall beside it. She wasn't going back to her room until she found it.

The sound of approaching footsteps from the room behind her nearly stopped her heart. She swirled her light over the long narrow sculpture gallery she just entered. Rows of rigid marble busts resting on tall ionic columns marched down the walls on both sides. She stepped behind the thickest column, flicked off the flashlight, and waited. Rapid steps *clickety clack, clickety clack,* on the stone floor came closer.

"Who's in here? You'd might as well come out at once. You jolly well know you're in here against the rules," rumbled a male voice. It held a strange mushy quality in what sounded like an attempt at disguise. With further distortion by the room's hollow echo, it gave Julia no inkling who the man was. She held her breath. Surely security people would not disguise their voices.

The man carried a small flashlight no more efficient than her own, which he held quite low and away from his body so that it did nothing to light his face. The narrow beam gyrated over the sculptures in a rapid succession of circular motions as he moved about the room.

A cold chill washed over Julia. A sudden impulse told her to step from her hiding place, light the man's face, and confess to her snooping. She was a member of the family, wasn't she? She was allowed to go anywhere she wanted to. Yet something stopped her. She hunched closer to the column as though the cold armless bust might come to life, realize her peril, and sprout arms to engulf her.

Whoever the intruder was, he was standing near her, for she could hear his quick breath. She was paralyzed with fear and could not force herself to peer around the column. Finally the footsteps moved into the distance and she found the courage to peek out in time to see the beam of light disappear through a door at the far end of the gallery. The door closed with a heavy *thunk*.

She tried to step from behind the sculpture but her foot would not move. She hugged the sculpture so closely that the buckle on her shoe was caught between the floor and a ridge at the base of the column. She turned her foot this way and that to dislodge it. Some friend this hollow-eyed fellow turned out to be.

Impatiently she kicked forward as hard as the space would allow. *Thwack!* The buckle came loose, and with a *zing* and a series of metallic clinks it shot across the floor like a guided missile. She stopped and stared with horror into the darkness. She debated whether she should take the time to look for it. She was not anxious to have it found in a place where she was not supposed to be. But she had no idea in which direction the buckle might have gone. No, she must let it go. She must get away before her stalker returned. She'd try to look for it tomorrow. She switched on her flashlight and made her way to the door the unknown intruder went through. Was he waiting for her on the other side like a playful cat waits for a mouse?

She pushed the heavy door open and swished her light around yet another cavernous room. Relief flooded over her. Here was the great hall she was looking for. Now she remembered the knights on horseback and the medieval suits of armor. Why didn't she figure it out? The oldest portion of the castle was arranged in a circle, one room flowing into another around a central courtyard.

Immediately she found the marble fireplace, ducked under the rope, and promptly stumbled over the dais, painfully bruising her right knee. She hardly felt it. She was already focusing her beam of light on the branding irons, eight in all, the long thin handles worn smooth from use.

The Celtic cross was third from the left end. She quickly examined the others--a crown, a grail, a horse's head, a Welsh knot, a headpiece for a suit of armor, a young woman's face. One was a shape she did not recognize.

She went back to the Celtic cross. There was no doubt about it, the scar on Paul Hampton's arm was made by this very branding iron. Paul Hampton was really her cousin, Nigel Maltby, no two ways about it. But why was he keeping his identity hidden from her?

Suddenly she panicked at the darkness and blanched at the knowledge that her cousin had ulterior motives in inviting her here. She scurried across the room, stumbling again on the dais, the light beam swinging erratically around the walls as she frantically sought a way out. Before her, double doors led into the front hall. She remembered it now, the black-and-white marble-tiled floor, the huge metal chandelier with warm softened candles leaning every which way over the wide stone staircase.

Off the hall was the dining room where, just an hour earlier, she dined with the other guests. Remnants of food odors clung to the cooling air. The skeletal remains of a fire still sputtered and sizzled in the fireplace, casting orange shards of light that melted into the high vaulted ceiling.

The main staircase was wider and more regular than the one she had mistakenly gone down earlier. When the pale light from the dining room fireplace no longer lit her way she switched on the flashlight again. Two large tallow candles, one on either side of the landing, put out a pale flickering glow that skittered soft angled shadows across the walls and doorways like dancing ghosts. Now, where was her room?

She recognized the wider of the two stone-paved corridors leading to the bedroom suites. The long passage was even more silent, cold and empty than she remembered. She whipped around at the sound of a sharp metallic click behind her and gawked openmouthed into the darkness near the bottom of the stairs. There was nothing.

In terror she fled to her room and slammed the lock into place. To her surprise someone had been there while she was away and built a fire in the tiny fireplace. Had Cousin Nigel paid her a visit after all?

Chapter 8

Mae Eldred tiptoed daintily, one foot carefully in front of the other like a nervous cat, down the steps to the dining room. She left her red wool blazer hanging on the back of her chair after dinner. She shivered as she remembered the guide who conducted the castle tour like a top sergeant earlier in the day. His dire warnings regarding where guests could or could not go, delivered via a commanding bullfrog voice, made a lasting impression on his hearers.

Ever since her activities in the underground during the war, Mae had been a rule follower. Life in those days was fraught with danger. She certainly did not want to be caught breaking Lord Maltby's rigid laws at Gorlachen, but it was her own jacket, wasn't it? She had been frozen ever since she arrived at the castle. If Lord Maltby didn't like her coming downstairs maybe he should consider heating the bloody frigid place. Shifting the blame to him gave her new courage. She threw her shoulders back indignantly, like parading before a group of snooping unsuspecting Nazis, and entered the room.

The dishes were cleared away and the room tidied. Trace odors of spicy foods and rich black coffee still lingered in the air. Fiery coals in the fireplace bathed the room with an ephemeral orange blush while they hissed and sputtered to a near death. The welcome heat embraced her as she crossed the mammoth Persian rug to the table.

The great expanse of the room was less friendly without talkative bickering guests. It seemed to vibrate with quiet, as though Mae's presence were disturbing and the room wanted to warn her away. She often had that same feeling during the war. It was a second sense one developed in life and death situations. She quickly learned to trust the warnings fully. They came, she knew, not from instinct, but from actual noises picked up on a subconscious level.

She stopped abruptly. There were voices behind her. They were not voices spoken aloud, but angry waves of hot coarse whispers. Was it security looking for her? Why should they be so angry?

Fear of getting into trouble prompted her to move quickly. She snatched her blazer from the chair, rushed across the room, and jerked open the door of a tall armoire, the only thing she could see that was quite large enough to get into. She stepped inside and pulled the door to.

Total blackness kept her from making out details, but the cupboard felt much larger than it looked from the outside. She hovered near the crack in the door and peered solemnly at busy figures who seemed to be wrestling in the passage near the dining room door. The shadowy darkness kept her from making out who they were or what they were actually doing.

She waited, her arms numbed with cold, until the angry whispers subsided. Whoever they were, they obviously were not looking for her. After what seemed like an eternity, she opened the door a few inches, stuck her head out, and peered cautiously around the room. She stepped from the cabinet and turned to latch the door.

"Oh," she nearly shouted aloud and jumped back. She couldn't have been more surprised if she were suddenly confronted by a man-eating tiger. A log in the fireplace shifted and lit the interior of the cabinet. It only appeared to be an armoire. She studied the cabinet doors inside and out. They camouflaged a narrow unlit stairway that rose steeply to some other area of the castle. But what part of the castle was it? She tried to recall the arrangement of rooms from the tour. It eluded her.

She paused in awe and gaped into the silent darkness above. A wild urge to follow the steps, to satisfy some primal curiosity that lurked with elusive dangers and thrills, teased the inner reaches of her brain. She had once been an adventurous sort. Why did she hesitate now? But why fool herself? She knew the answer. It was because she was used to John being too protective, always telling her what to do.

40

Mae and John Eldred met as very young teenagers running errands for the Dutch underground during the war. Their work together was a grueling life-threatening experience. When the war ended and they were married, John became an overly-protective husband who felt compelled to keep his sweet innocent wife's delicate eyes and ears from any further harsh realities of life. There were times when Mae could have brained him from sheer frustration. As he aged he became increasingly less concerned about his appearance--his coat was often sprinkled with dandruff, his hair sometimes resembled a bristling bird's nest, and it wasn't the least bit unusual for her to discover him wearing unmatched socks or a necktie that, in color, had no relationship whatever to the rest of his clothes. Did excessive drinking lead to unimaginative thinking or an inability to deal with life's unusual happenings that called for opinions besides his own?

Mae did not want to be sweet and innocent. Innocence was for children. She wanted to be a woman in her own right. Today she felt a new sense of dissatisfaction when she met and talked with Jeannie Quayle.

Jeannie worked with her husband, but was independent of constant advice and criticism as to how to pursue the writing of the travel book. He had enough faith in her intelligence to allow her to go about it in her own way. Mae knew that if she tried to write a book, or do anything else for that matter, John would take it over and tell her exactly how to do it. She highly resented his attitude.

She looked longingly up the steps. Perhaps she should take this opportunity to do something secret and forbidden on her own. She stepped back into the armoire and closed the door to see if it might help her make a decision. Her eye was abruptly drawn again to the light through the crack. Someone passed very quietly by the dining room door on their way up the main staircase. Who were all of these people prowling about in the dark?

She hesitated. Her heart beat wildly, erratically. She was torn between a feverish desire to follow the hidden passage into the unknown, and going back to her husband's arms while minding her own business.

Somewhere above her a door opened, creating a draft that made her shiver. The floor creaked under scuffling footsteps. Was someone coming down the stairs? In panic she jumped through the door of the armoire, slammed it, leaving a hollow clicking echo in its wake, and fled to the upstairs hall with an energy she had not possessed in years.

What was the pounding she heard? She swung around and peered into the darkness at the foot of the stairs. Finally she realized the hammering was her own heart. Or was it?

Julia nearly jumped out of her skin at the unexpected knock on her bedroom door. Had security followed her? She was about to ignore it-- she wasn't interested in defending herself against security--when it came again, an urgent sharp rap from a woman's hand. She paused a moment, trying to decide what to do. Was it Rachel?

"Who is it?" she asked quietly.

"Mae Eldred," a frantic voice whispered, "Please, let me in."

When Julia opened the door the woman nearly fell into her arms. Mae recovered her balance and quickly closed and locked the door.

"I...I think someone is following me," Mae said. Her breath came in great gulps. Her dark puckered eyes stared harshly into the lamplight. "I went down to the dining room to get a blazer I left on the back of my chair after dinner. Oh, I know I wasn't supposed to be down there. When I turned into the dining room I heard someone behind me. Then some people who seemed to be angry with each other came by the door and disappeared into the great hall." She looked sheepish, as though her story were so weird no one could possibly believe it. "I was so afraid of being caught I hid behind a door. But when I came back up the stairs I think someone followed me. That's why I stopped here."

Julia took hold of the babbling woman's thick fleshy arm and set her down in a chair near the fire.

"There now," she said soothingly, trying to calm herself as well as Mae. Didn't she run into something similar? "Surely we're in friendly company. I can't imagine why anyone would find it necessary to follow you in a secretive way."

She saw me, Julia suddenly realized, grateful that Mae obviously could not identify her. "I suspect it was a security person keeping an eye on you. He saw you pick up your own jacket and come back upstairs with it, so he decided not to make a thing of it. That's all there is to it. Now let me walk you back to your room. You'll feel better after a good night's sleep."

"I...I guess so," Mae said reluctantly. "I'm beginning to distrust this place."

You said it, Julia thought, but this was no time to burden Mae with her own doubts. It would only add to her fears. The two walked down the long corridor arm in arm. Julia gazed at the long stone passage with its inadequate medieval lighting and wondered who had walked these halls in generations before her. More Maltbys with their odd secretive ways?

The Eldred's room was next to Rachel's on the end facing the courtyard. When Mae entered the room and closed the door behind her Julia turned back to her own room.

With a quick jerk Mae's door flew open again and she was back in the hall beside Julia. "John's not here," she whimpered. "Where do you suppose he could have got to? He was in the shower when I left."

Julia sighed. In spite of the fact that she knew Mae was on edge, she was tired and wanted to get to bed where she could think. The Eldreds would have to settle their own problems.

"He'll surely be back soon," she said to Mae, and hurried away to avoid further involvement.

Chapter 9

Julia could not remember how she got through the first part of the night, but by half past eight the following morning she was awake and alert. She pulled herself upright under the tester on her grandmother's bed and savored the feminine elegance of the room.

It was a different world from the rest of the austere castle. However, its rosy Victorian beauty did nothing for the damp cold that pervaded it. She forgot to close the window before she went to bed. An ice cold wind from the North Sea blew the delicate lace curtains aside and revealed a gray sodden sky. She frowned at the thought of more rain. She so looked forward to a beautiful day to visit Dunrose Manor.

She just scrambled down from the ridiculously high bed when a heavy-handed banging on the door shattered her journey into the thoughtful delights of old manor houses. She looked around for her robe, then realized she was so busy after her arrival yesterday she didn't take the time to unpack her heavy bag. Being a worry wart by nature she had tucked a new gauzy white nightie into her carryon just in case the airline lost her luggage, but she didn't included a robe.

The insistent pounding came again.

"Who is it?" she called irritably while she tried to open the catch on her case. She sat down on it to further mash the lid down to help release the catch and gave a valiant tug. It was hopeless. It was simply stuffed too full.

"Nigel Maltby," said a formal voice beyond the door.

"Just a sec. I'm trying to get my robe."

He knocked briskly again. "I must talk to you immediately. Open the door, please."

The ring of authority in his voice startled Julia. Not only did her cousin disguise himself from her yesterday, but his replacement was behaving in a most ungentlemanly manner. If he was going to reprimand her for her trip downstairs last night he was not going to have the last word with her.

She gave up on the suitcase, and in frustration lifted the lock on the door and peered into the murky passage. "What's so urgent? I understood breakfast is available until half past nine," she said.

The man who disguised himself as Nigel Maltby leaned against the wall opposite her door with his arms folded across his chest as though he was prepared to stand there, pounding on the door intermittently, all day if necessary. He wore a dark green long-sleeved shirt and blue jeans. He didn't bother to say good morning."There's an emergency," he said in a brisk tone, his dark red eyes leveled on hers with concern. "All guests and servants must be gathered in the dining room within fifteen minutes."

"Let's see. What could possibly be considered an emergency at Castle Gorlachen?" Julia yawned, rubbed her eyes, then pointed a finger at him. "I know. You found a spot of tarnish on the bell that summons the servants to your side."

His eyes opened wide while he studied her, as though trying to figure out what he was letting himself in for.

"Or maybe the cook quit in a huff without so much as a by your leave, and you've learned that we must all hunt our own pheasant and scramble our own eggs?" she said mercilessly.

"Believe me, this is no laughing matter," he chided. "I must restore order at Gorlachen."

"I see. Well, if it's order you want, you'd better come in and open my suitcase, *cuz*, or I won't have a thing to put on." She waited for a reaction to her emphasis on the cuz, but he merely brushed past her into the room in a businesslike way and jerked the catch loose on her case. As he turned, his eyes swept over her and missed nothing of the revealing filmy nightgown.

45

In the sparring contest, Julia completely forgot her lack of a robe. She grabbed a coverlet and pulled it around her shoulders.

"Get some clothes on," he said. "We don't need any more trouble."

"Thank you, Cousin Nigel," she said cattily. She was onto their little joke. She was not going to let her cousin or his ill-cast friend off easily. "I assure you I'll be quite adequately dressed when I appear at your very important meeting."

As he stepped into the hall, two uniformed police officers walked briskly past them, both carrying paper coffee cups, and both intent on whatever it was they had on their minds. One managed a brief smile at Julia, and both tipped their heads slightly to the man whom they probably thought was the Lord of Gorlachen.

Julia looked after the officers in wonder. Surely a game wouldn't include the police.

"What's the big emergency? You never did say," she called after her red-eyed nemesis.

"There's been a murder in the sculpture gallery," he said without looking around.

Julia gaped in dismay as he disappeared into the dismal interior of the castle. She felt as though she was acting in a dream as she pulled gray wool slacks and a pink Shetland wool pullover from her suitcase. She was thoroughly chilled both from the weather and the unhappy prospect of murder. Who was with her in the sculpture gallery last night, and why? Was this another of cousin Nigel's practical jokes to make her stay seem medieval? Something on the order of Duncan and Macbeth? Perhaps he had known she was the one hiding in the gallery and intended to make a fool of her over it. Her brain reeled with unanswered questions. It was all too far-fetched to grasp. She wouldn't be surprised if there were no murder at all.

She ran a brush through her snarled hair, smoothed on glossy pink lipstick, and welcomed the warmth of cashmere knee socks that matched her sweater. She meant to put on the black pumps she left by the bed last night when she changed for her late tour of the castle, but somehow her foot would not slide into the left shoe. She shoved her leg forward to force her foot into it. It simply would not go. She studied the shoe, then shrugged as she reached down to pull it on. It was no use.

She picked it up and examined it. A hard round object was jammed solidly into the toe. She worked it back and forth with numb fingers to dislodge it. Out popped an opaque thirty-five millimeter film container. She pulled the lid off and stared blankly at a roll of film.

Chapter 10

When Rachel saw Julia enter the dining room she waved from across the room, then turned her full attention back to a conversation with Jeremy Andrews. Sara, looking coolly elegant as usual in a hot pink jump suit with matching sandals, sat beside them gazing sleepily into space, paying little attention to anything in particular.

Seated at the long dining table, John Eldred ran his fingers slowly up and down Mae's arm, lightly fondling her breast with each pass, while Mae sat perfectly still and seemed to glare into the fire, her sleep-worn face taking on a forlorn look. Navy blue slacks and a baggy brown tweed sweater that looked two sizes too large seemed hastily thrown together. When she saw Julia she jumped up and rushed across the room.

"They're going to think I did it, aren't they?" she said, her mouth turned down at the corners as though she had been sentenced to hang.

"You mean because you were down here last night?" Julia said. "How are they going to know unless you tell them? I'm certainly not going to tell them anything. I don't even know what's going on."

"Shouldn't they know I saw those people wrestling through the door of the great hall?"

Julia studied Mae's worried face.

"I wouldn't say anything if I were you, Mae. Why complicate matters for yourself?" She wondered if Mae was one of those people who simply could not refrain from telling the full truth no matter what was at stake. "I

48

feel quite sure that whatever happened down here last night has nothing at all to do with any of us. Let's wait and see what it's all about."

"Poor Professor Quayle. We hardly had a chance to get acquainted," Mae said sadly.

Julia wheeled around to look at her. "Professor Quayle? You mean someone murdered the Professor?" Julia's breath caught in her throat. Somehow she expected either no murder at all, or at least a victim she never heard of--a nosy gardener, a pregnant unmarried servant, or, perhaps, an overzealous butler. Obviously she had read too many English mystery novels.

A chill that had nothing at all to do with the weather shook her violently as the grim realization of her involvement became clear. It had to be Professor Quayle's film container in her shoe. Who else's could it be? And why put it in *her* shoe? He was the only one allowed to take pictures inside, her cousin said. But what could it have to do with her? A gray curtain dropped slowly over her eyes. She dropped onto a chair and tried to steady herself.

Julia stared numbly into the concerned blue-gray eyes of the man she now knew to be her cousin. They were shaped like her own and nearly the same color. He made her take a drink of water and bathed her forehead with a cloth. *What is he trying to do to me? Whatever it is, it's gone too far.*

"I'm quite all right, Mr. Hampton, thank you." She shrugged his hands away and used his assumed name. She intended to keep him in his place as a guest on an equal footing with herself until she revealed her knowledge of his true identity. She picked up her purse and began to sort through it for a handkerchief.

In a flurry of officiousness and bad humor, Nigel's red-eyed stand-in and a tall thin detective in his early fifties, whipped through the room and stopped importantly at the head of the table.

The Inspector set down a notebook, pen, and a small automatic camera. His damp Harris tweed jacket and slightly rumpled gray trousers reeked of wool, tobacco, and saltwater air. An odor of sweet hair tonic hung about him. Raindrops clinging to thin gray hair glistened like fiery opals against the red coals of the fireplace, lending him a devilish air.

Julia studied him with concern. His face was long and thin and creased with a web of fine wrinkles like a well-used soft leather glove. His expression seemed hard, a little arrogant Julia thought, as he lifted a lean pointed chin to the group as though to say, *I'm going to be here for a while, if you don't like it, get used to it.* Julia shook her head over all the things that have happened since she arrived at Gorlachen. She leaned back in her chair and wondered what could possibly happen next.

The servants, twelve in all, filed into the room. Red Eyes--Julia knew no other name for him--signaled for quiet. The eyes took in every detail of the group. Somehow he managed to avoid looking directly at Julia.

"My friend and guests of Gorlachen," he began. "I'm sorry to have to inconvenience you in this way, but I think you all know by now that Professor Quayle was found dead this morning--murdered as it were--in the lower floor sculpture gallery. Chief Inspector Henry Walpole, from the Walthorpe CID, has arrived from the mainland to take charge of the investigation. I'm sure you'll want to give him your full cooperation in solving this sordid affair." His eyes finally swept over Julia as though to satisfy himself that she did, indeed, put on more appropriate clothes. He stepped aside and relinquished the floor to the inspector.

Walpole began to pace back and forth behind the high-backed chairs, his damp brown shoes squeaking slightly with each pass.

"Well, there you 'ave it," he said solemnly and gazed over the group. The face he turned to them seemed set in stone. "It appears that Mr. Quayle was battered about the 'ead with a heavy object which has not yet been found. The time of death is set by the coroner at approximately half past ten last night." He thrust his chin up and forward when he spoke and wheezed slightly as though he had tried to swallow a chunk of meat too large for his gullet.

"Now," he said, turning protruding watery blue eyes on the group. "Can anyone in this room shed light on the matter?" The light of his eyes seemed to fluctuate in intensity as they moved from one person to the next, as though sizing up the enormity of the situation, while he waited for an answer.

Indecision raced frantically through Julia's brain. Should she admit her presence in the gallery before he found out some other way? Her hand nearly went up, then she abruptly dropped it to her side. The man looked so formidable she could not bring herself to do it.

"Someone tried to rape my wife down here last night," John Eldred said in a sudden fit of passion while waving his hand over those present.

Surprised gasps filled the room. Heads turned in unison to study Mae.

Mae looked at her husband futilely and sighed, as though the last thing she wanted was for John to become involved.

"Now see here, Eldred," Jeremy Andrews said nastily, "are you implying that one of us present here this morning tried to rape your wife? That, my good man, is wishful thinking on your part."

"I beg your pardon," John bristled. He cupped his fingers under Mae's chin and pulled her face up to look into his eyes. "Beauty has always been in the eye of the beholder."

"Yes. Well thank God for that," Jeremy said and turned away to stare resentfully into the fire.

Sara Danes, forever aware of her looks, ran her hands down her fitted jumpsuit in a provocative way and moved closer to Jeremy to slip her hand into his.

"Tell us what 'appened, Mrs. Eldred." Not even Sara Danes's good looks distracted Walpole's steady gaze from Mae.

"Well...." Mae looked warily at John as though he were a dangerous animal ready to charge, and looked over at Julia as though hoping she might back up her story.

"I want to 'ear it from you, Mrs. Eldred," Walpole said stonily.

"You can jolly well talk to me." John jumped unsteadily to his feet. "I'm her husband. She'll need me to keep the facts straight. I can tell you whatever it is you need to know for both of us."

Walpole's cold gaze flicked over John like a quick lick with a swatter, then settled again on Mae.

"Yes, Mrs. Eldred? You were not a witness to the act, Mr. Eldred. Please sit down."

John wobbled backwards, nearly missing his chair.

"It was about ten o'clock," Mae said quietly. She gave John an

51

apologetic look, then settled into what appeared to be a fully determined desire to recall exactly what took place. "John and I had gone to our room for the night. It was miserably cold. When I went to the armoire for my blazer I realized I left it hanging on the back of my dining chair at dinner. I couldn't see what harm it would do if I came downstairs to get it. It belongs to me after all," she snitted. 'If the Lord of Gorlachen doesn't like it, maybe he should try heating this bloody place.

"Oh, I know I wasn't supposed to be down here. That nasty little tour guide with the strident voice threatened us over it like he was expecting us to behave like a bunch of common criminals," she spat. "When I got inside the dining room, I heard footsteps in the hall. I was so frightened of being caught by security that I stepped behind a door where I couldn't be seen."

Julia cringed as all eyes turned to examine the massive oak door that closed the dining room from the main hall.

"In a little bit, some figures passed in the hall and disappeared into that big room over there." Mae pointed to the entrance to the great hall.

"Did you recognize the figures?" Walpole asked.

"I could hardly see them. It was quite dark." Mae glared spitefully at the guests gathered around the table as though they were the cause of her unfortunate involvement. She gave Jeremy Andrews a particularly nasty look. "I don't know any of these disgusting people anyway."

The group all shook their heads as though the Eldreds were a lost cause and wondered what else was coming.

"How many figures were there?" Walpole carped.

"I don't know," she addressed him with more than a trace of annoyance. "Like I said, I was behind the door. A person can't see through a door now, can they?"

"I need specifics, Mrs. Eldred. You actually saw someone, or you *thought* you saw someone?"

"I did see someone."

"More than one person?" Walpole held Mae's eyes with his in a soul-searching gaze.

"Well, I...yes. There was more than one. I remember now. I heard whispers."

"You 'eard these people whispering then?"

"Yes, as they went by the door. They whispered like they were very angry."

"And what was being said, eh, Mrs. Eldred?"

John Eldred jumped to his feet again like a defendant's lawyer pleading irrelevance. "She's already told you every bloody thing she knows, Walpole. If she hadn't come down here to get her jacket, which is no bloody business of yours anyway, you wouldn't have known there were whispers, would you? Why don't you pick on some of these others for a while? I ran onto every bloody one of them down here last night." He looked over the group. "Those two over there," he said, pointing out Jeremy Andrews and Sara Danes. "I passed them coming up the stairs about midnight."

"Yes, the servants explained that Andrews and Sara Danes were downstairs looking for aspirin," Walpole said. "Now, what 'appened after the figures disappeared from the hall, Mrs. Eldred? You have yet to tell us of the attempted rape."

It was clear Walpole had no intention of allowing John Eldred to get the better of him. He waited while Mae collected her thoughts regarding her husband's claim of attempted rape.

"Well, I...I hurried up the steps. Near the top I thought I heard someone behind me...."

The room vibrated with tension as the guests hung on her every word. Who among them had tried to rape Mae Eldred?

Apparently the attention prompted Mae to turn dramatic. "I turned about in a sudden sweeping gesture and peered desperately into the darkness below, but there was nothing, no one at all. It turned out to be the pounding of my own heart."

The guests, who waited in paralyzed wonder, let out deep breaths, made disappointed grimaces, and leaned back against their chairs as they looked at Mae with disgust.

Walpole digested this last bit of information. "And?"

"And nothing," Mae said. "Nothing else happened. I went to our room to find John, but he wasn't there."

"Are you telling us there was no attempted rape then? And where was your husband?" Walpole asked, leaning toward her as though to pull the information from her with the magnetism of his own body.

"Well, I...I don't know. I didn't ask. When you know your husband admires other women as mine does, you don't ask where he's been. You don't want to know, do you? He came back later and we went to bed."

"Where were you, Mr. Eldred?"

"He was in my room, at least part of the time," Rachel chimed in. There were surprised guffaws and raised eyebrows around the table.

"I thought so," Mae said, shaking her head up and down knowingly while looking at Rachel with malice.

"It's not what you think, Mrs. Eldred," Rachel said quickly, her face flushing scarlet. "Your husband discovered you were missing and came to see if you were in my room. I'm just next door. I asked him to help me with the fire I was having difficulty getting started, which he did, and then he left to try to find you."

Julia read total disgust for Rachel in Mae Eldred's eyes. In spite of her domineering husband, the woman obviously possessed more than a little grit.

"When your 'usband returned to the room, did you tell him someone had tried to rape you?" Walpole asked.

"No." She avoided John's eyes. "He came to that conclusion on his own. When I told him about the people in the hall, he said, 'only men looking for available women potter about a castle in the dark.' Those were his exact words. He often thinks other men are making passes at me. Believe me, it's been a long time since anyone has."

Meaningful glances and knowing smiles were exchanged around the table.

John obviously missed none of it. He blinked several times as though to clear away the milky haze from early morning tippling and found Walpole's gaze newly directed at him.

"Mr. Eldred? I'm only trying to get the facts here, you understand. Attempted rape is a serious charge."

"Early on I happened to be taking a shower, if that's what you call that bloody anemic trickle of water. When I finished, my wife was gone.

She mentioned earlier that she left her jacket downstairs, but knowing her sense of direction, she could wander through this whole bloody castle trying to find her way back to the room. She's given that way, you know. Sometimes I'm up to my eyes with it." He rubbed his forehead to get a grip on himself. "But after I left Miss Givens's room, could I find her? No, that's what. I have no doubt one of these romeos took the opportunity to have some pleasure at my expense. Enjoy, enjoy," he ranted spitefully.

Mae jumped to her feet, her face drained of color. "I refuse to listen to this nonsense any longer. Why don't you tell them what you were *really* doing in Rachel's room last night, John? I've watched your eyes rove over all of these young women since we arrived here. What you had on your mind didn't fool me one bit. Do you think I didn't see you trying to look under the housemaid's skirts when she bent over to set the fire last night?"

"Mae, my darling, what has come over you? I...."

"It wasn't that way at all, Mrs. Eldred," Rachel interrupted, but the look she got in return from Mae shut her up, as though pursuing the matter would only draw her in deeper.

Walpole amazed Julia. He waited patiently to break in, as though, under the stress of investigation, all husbands and wives had similar exchanges. True feelings erupted, and the couple ended up with either a better understanding of one another or they headed straight for the divorce courts.

"Well now," Walpole said, looking over the group, apparently deciding to ignore the gouging couple, "I'll see you individually later. Should you remember anything at all about last night, please report to me or to Lord Maltby immediately." No doubt he planned to catch up with the Eldreds in their room where they could continue their marital bashing in private. The remainder of the guests were awed to complete silence by the marital tiff.

Julia watched Walpole's eyes narrow into a concentrated glitter as he surveyed the tense faces around him. As time went by he would have a chance to become acquainted with each and every one of them. He probably was already separating them into categories, some capable of murder, some not. Julia wondered into which category he placed her.

"You may have your breakfast now," Walpole said finally. "Of course, no one will be allowed to leave the premises until everyone 'as been questioned and released."

"Just one more thing," Nigel's double spoke up. "Does anyone claim this buckle? It appears to have come from a shoe. It was found in the sculpture gallery near Professor Quale's body."

Julia stared at the object in horror. It was the buckle from her soft-soled shoes. She studied the man who held it, the man with intrepid red eyes who was obviously ready to shout "murderer" to whoever claimed it. She was not about to speak up.

A formally dressed butler whom Julia hadn't seen before appeared in the dining room door.

"Breakfast is suved, my Lowd," he announced in a pompous British tone.

"Wow. How's that for medieval? An honest-to-God murder right here in the midst of us. Cousin Nigel couldn't have planned it better." Rachel breezed in beside Julia and appeared to be delighted with the prospects.

"That's disgusting," Julia wheezed. "I must say you have a strange sense of humor, Rachel."

"Excuuuuse me," Rachel threw up her hands in a futile gesture. "I forgot we're still mourning cousin Nigel's lack of attention."

"There's more to it than you know," Julia whimpered.

"Tell me about it while we have breakfast. I'm starving." She studied Julia's face. "You look like death warmed over, honey. What's happened to you?"

"Everything has gone wrong," Julia said, bursting into tears.

"It can't be as bad as all that." Rachel hugged her close. "Tell Aunt Rachel about it."

They followed the butler into an attractive small breakfast room brightened by a set of four floor-to-ceiling stone-mullioned windows. A long Chippendale buffet loaded with delicious-smelling food sparkled with stacks of gold-rimmed plates and row upon row of silver service.

Julia picked up a knife, fork, and spoon, and left the other odd-shaped pieces for those who knew what to do with them. Even though she had eaten little the night before, she could not work up an appetite. She took a small helping of some sort of gray mealy-looking cooked cereal, a slice of dark toast, and coffee.

Rachel loaded her plate with a taste of everything in sight and settled herself happily by Julia at a narrow trestle table covered with a white cloth. "What's going on, Julia? Why the long face? Are you really feeling that bad over the death of a man you didn't even know?"

"Rachel, my God, we're talking about *murder.* We don't know who did it or who might be next. Doesn't that frighten you even a little?"

"It doesn't have anything to do with us. Can't you see, Julia? None of us knew Quayle when we came here. Why would we want to murder him? I must admit the thought crossed my mind when he continued his unsought lecture about the food at dinner last night, but I resisted the temptation. Be reasonable, hon. With Inspector Walpole here to take charge the case will be solved in no time."

Julia stared at her friend in exasperation. She must take into account that Rachel knew nothing of the film canister left in her shoe. "You've been reading too many mystery novels, Rachel. And if it's the jewels you've come to see, I'm afraid we won't be seeing them. My cousin obviously is not going to give me the time of day while I'm here."

"Have you talked to him about it? What's wrong with him, anyway? Why is he behaving so strangely after he invited you here to look at the jewelry?" Rachel stuffed her mouth with sweet dark bread.

"I wish I knew the answers," Julia said thoughtfully. She wanted desperately to confide in Rachel, to tell her the man who called himself Paul Hampton was really her cousin, Nigel Maltby, but she had to prove to herself first that she was correct about it. What could she do to flush Nigel out?

Chapter 11

By the time breakfast was over the rain had stopped, but a gray sky, hanging in tatters like Persian cat hair, threatened to inundate the island again. While the guests learned medieval parlor games in the library, Julia let herself through the security gate and struck out across the classic perennial garden.

Drifts of delicious color and sweet elusive scents were intensified in the heavy sullenness of the damp morning. She stopped to take it all in. She was standing near a small pond surrounded by robust plants blooming with vivid colors. Koi glided and cavorted near the surface of the water. From a high rock wall a lion's-head lavabo gushed a fine spray that resembled the hissing of feline fear. Julia waved to it as a kindred spirit. She understood the feeling well.

She made a mental note to spend some time in the garden to take in its enchanted beauty. After all, beautiful gardens were her heritage, weren't they? Her father had always given the English garden extravagant praise. But it would have to wait for another time. She felt she must hurry along the cliff to the path leading down the steep rocky slope where a well-trimmed lawn fell away from the garden on all sides.

Once past the garden she turned her full attention to the country house looming in the distance that she thought must be Dunrose Manor.

The house, built from the same local stone as the castle, stretched across the grounds in a series of additions fanning out from a fourteenth-century pele tower. Three clusters of tall handsome chimneys with saucy twisted chimney pots stood proudly on a later addition. Julia simply did not have the time or the inclination to keep the architectural periods straight in her head.

The path curved around natural stone outcroppings. She stopped in a spot where she could look back to a full view of the castle. A roll of woolly gray morning mist hovered at the base of the rock. She peered into the cottony mass. Did she see something move? She studied the spot for a time, her heart pounding in her ears. A deep sense of unease pricked at her thoughts. She whirled around to look behind her. Seeing nothing she turned and ran for the manor house.

As she got closer, her fears lessened and she was pleased to see that the house was in better condition than her cousin's photograph suggested. The upper portions of the castle were reflected in stone-mullioned windows. The reflection loomed threateningly over her approach as though it had raced her to the spot to leer and glower at her.

A wide gravel path led to a stone stairwell and onto a formal stone-paved verandah. Massive double oak doors looked impenetrable. She pulled on the handles with all her strength, but they refused to give. High shuttered windows facing the verandah didn't allow even a glimpse inside.

She left the verandah and followed the gravel path that continued around the outside of the house to the back. The house was considerably larger than it appeared from the front, unfolding in added-on layers, making the trip around it a distance ordeal in itself.

She rounded the back corner and came to a sudden stop. She was about to step into a paradise, a riotous explosion of shimmering purple, pink, and white roses. Situated among trellises, fountains, and pergolas, provocative Italian marble statues and giant urns interspersed with gravel paths led the eye to a low stone wall grandly draped with even more colorful blooms. A spicy fragrance filled the air. Julia gazed around her. Someone obviously cared deeply about the place.

A side path led to a back entrance. The door opened easily, letting out a stream of warm air. Cautiously she peered into the hall. Seeing no one, she pushed the door wider.

"Hello," she called into a bright yellow high-roofed hallway. She listened for a time. There was no answer. She moved further inside. The hall led into a dark tudor-paneled parlor filled with mellow old furniture arranged attractively around an orange, brown and black Bohkara rug. Remains of a fire sputtered in a rather crude stone fireplace flanked by grinning stone Maltby lions. A low-key red, tan, and dark brown color scheme could only be described as thoroughly masculine.

"Hellooo," she called again. "Anybody home?"

To the left was a small well-designed kitchen with modern oak cabinets and the latest dark red appliances. A dishwasher hummed through its cycle.

Julia crossed the room and followed a wide staircase to the upper story. Would someone accuse her of breaking and entering? She certainly could not count on backing from cousin Nigel, but she was mesmerized by the warmth and comfort of the place. She couldn't resist it, and wasn't it hers?

She came into a wide, airy, upstairs hallway that ran the full length of what appeared to be the most recent addition. There were at least a dozen doors leading from it. All were closed but one. Timidly she entered the enormous room. It occurred to her at that moment that it was the most beautiful bedroom she had ever laid eyes on.

A massive ancient bed canopied with a heavy fabric printed with medieval hunt scenes dominated one side of the room. Matching Chippendale lowboys on either side served as night tables. Delicate white-on-white garland wallpaper was topped by rich mahogany paneling on the high ceiling. Julia stood perfectly still and gazed at the lovely room.

Suddenly she jumped at the sight of her own eyes gazing back at her from a photograph among several others on one of the lowboys. It was small, five-by-seven inches, taken two years ago shortly before her parents were killed. Her father must have sent it. One of the photographs was of her grandmother. Another was her mother and father's wedding picture. There was a pale, thin-haired man who resembled her father. Nigel's father? There were several others whom she did not recognize.

She was lost in contemplation of the pictures when a soft sound behind her abruptly whirled her around.

60

He leaned casually against the door wearing pale blue linen slacks and a matching shirt and smiled shyly into her startled eyes. "Hello, Julia Maltby," he said pleasantly.

"Hello, Nigel Maltby." His smile was so contagious she had to return it. She immediately felt her face color with embarrassment at being caught snooping. "I...I don't know quite how to explain myself. I *had* to see Dunrose Manor. I couldn't go back to New York without...without seeing the manor house," she stumbled on as though any explanation she might give would not be believed.

"It's quite all right," he assured her. "It belongs to you. I'm glad you came here this morning. It gives us a chance to get acquainted." He looked her over purposefully. "You know, you're exactly what I thought you'd be. You're pretty and petite, and, according to reports from my thoroughly frustrated detective, Paul Hampton, you have the old Maltby spunk. How did you know I'm the real Nigel? Surely you didn't remember me from that early visit."

She thoughtfully looked him over, thoroughly puzzled. "No, I didn't remember you. The scar of the cross on your arm gave you away. My father, mother, and I shuddered over how it got there for years." Suddenly she felt flushed and giddy. Then she recalled what she had been up against since arriving at the castle and turned serious. "Now you explain to me why you invited me here only to hide your identity."

"Come down to the kitchen." He took her arm and led her down the stairs. "I noticed you didn't eat much breakfast. Let me fix you something while we talk."

"Have you been watching me?"

"Your every move," he grinned, "and I've enjoyed every moment of it."

"Do you live here?"

"I do, indeed. I've never liked living in the castle. It's too big, too formal, too busy, too cold. Dunrose Manor is a place where I have privacy and can be myself. I like my own cooking and I collect my own furniture. I do my own housework and gardening and I strictly forbid any of the castle staff to set foot on the place."

61

"Then what was all that business the guide told us about the family living quarters in the west wing of the castle?"

"It's true. My parents lived there, and I did too until about two years ago. I simply cannot stand hiding away in a stuffy apartment while tourists have the run of the place. How can you beat Dunrose Manor?"

The handsome smile captured her again. There was a resemblance to her father, but Nigel was better looking.

"For historical reasons I shall always keep the west wing of the castle exactly as it was while my parents lived there. I spend an hour or two a day in the castle office. Occasionally I wow my friends with a rock and roll blowout in the great hall. The bed and breakfast business is run by the servants. I have no patience with it at all."

"What about my father? Where did he live?"

"His quarters were on the top floor of the keep. He didn't get on well with the rest of the family. He was a different sort, as it were. He liked to stay to himself."

While one part of Julia's brain tried to figure out what would have been different about her father, the other insisted on flirting with the image of Nigel's slim hard body gyrating wildly to a rock and roll beat.

He put two thick slices of glossy brown bread in a toaster and heated mugs of coffee in the microwave. "I was planning to have you stay here at Dunrose Manor, but when the difficulties arose I gave it up. I felt grandmother's room in the keep was the next best choice. She lived part of the time in this house until she was unable to care for herself, then we moved her to the castle permanently. This place has been going steadily down hill ever since." He pulled the toast from the toaster, buttered it lightly, and set the dish on a butler's tray with the coffee.

"What difficulties?" Julia asked blankly.

Nigel set the tray on a Chippendale table in front of the fireplace. "Help yourself to the toast and I'll try to explain this very unpleasant situation." He set a cup of rich black coffee before her, then sat down with a heavy sigh as though he were at a loss to know how to begin.

Julia leaned comfortably in her chair and sipped coffee while she watched his gaze flit from one thing to another, then settle his gaze, reluctantly, on hers.

"When you wrote to say you were accepting my invitation to visit the castle, you mentioned you were bringing a friend along, one Rachel Givens. Her occupation was listed as gemologist. Considering the fact that you were to be given full range of the castle buildings and grounds as a member of the Maltby family, and considering the historical significance of Gorlachen and the need for tight security, I hired a detective, Paul Hampton, to run an FBI check on Rachel."

"You what?" Julia said, jumping forward in her chair with disbelief. "Hello? What on earth are you talking about?"

"There's no need to be upset about it. I often check out prospective guests if they appear to have some interest in Gorlachen that might prove untoward. Historical properties are regularly burglarized on the islands."

"And what did your little investigation produce?" Julia was scandalized that her friend was under such close scrutiny.

"Well, let's put it this way," he said, looking her squarely in the eye, "she didn't pass."

Julia sat perfectly still, her cup poised in midair. "I have no idea what you're talking about. Rachel is a good friend and a delightful person. Why, I think she wanted to see Gorlachen almost more than I did."

"I'm sure that's true," Nigel said dryly. "The fact is, Rachel Givens is a suspected jewel thief. Her name has been linked with two unsolved heists in the States. So far her involvement has not been proved, but investigations show she has been under surveillance by the FBI more than once."

Julia couldn't have been more insulted if he slapped her across the face. She set her cup down on the tray with deliberate care and rose from her chair. The heat of sudden fury drenched her body with perspiration.

"Is this some kind of game you're playing? Ever since I arrived here life has seemed like one big put-on. Do you know I really thought at the beginning that it was part of the medieval setup? That medieval lords were some kind of corny practical jokers? Well, I've just changed my mind. You're all crazy, that's it. You're stark-raving mad."

She got up from her chair and marched huffily to the door. "You were going to allow me to visit here for five days with your identity hidden? When were we going to talk about jewelry, Dunrose Manor, and the National Trust?" Her tone had taken a nasty turn. She marched out the door and stalked with determined anger up the gravel path.

Nigel stayed right on her heels. "Julia, wait. Please stay and talk to me. I need someone, can't you see that? By the time the FBI report came to us, you and Rachel were already on the plane bound for London. We thought it would work to place Paul Hampton as Lord of Gorlachen-- give him the freedom to go anywhere in the castle without suspicion. That way he could keep an eye on Rachel and the other guests without appearing to be watching them. I hoped the plan would free me to spend time with you if you wanted it that way. Please, come back."

Julia stopped and considered it. "What are we going to talk about, my good friend? Forget it." It was hard to resist needling him. He sounded so paranoid and put upon.

"I can never fully explain how sorry I am I chose to do it this way, for your sake and mine. The minute I saw you that first day I knew it was a bloody serious mistake. I should have set it right with you straightaway, and that's what I'm trying to do, damn it. Won't you come back and hear me out? We're dealing with murder here."

Julia turned a critical eye on him. The crisp blue shirt now draped dowdily over a braided belt. His face was flushed with emotion. Was he some kind of nut?

"Surely you don't think Rachel had something to do with Quayle's murder?" Julia's brain reeled with shocking unbelievable revelations. Rachel? A thief? A murderer? She slowly shook her head. "I must get back to my room. I don't believe I can quite comprehend it."

"Don't tell anyone my true identity. Will you do that much for me? It might work yet if the other guests are unaware of our knowledge, particularly Rachel."

"I may keep your absurd little secret and I may not," she said carelessly. What did she owe him after all of this inexplicable nonsense?

"Be careful, Julia." His voice turned flat and cold. "Don't play fast and loose with murder."

"Play?" She laughed with delight. "At least you've got that part right."

"Maybe you'd better hear something else while we're at it then, little Miss Know-it-all," he enunciated angrily.

Julia followed his suspicious glances around the grounds to make sure no one was within hearing.

"I'll bet you didn't know that Jeremy Andrews is Rachel Givens's husband."

Julia scoffed, but suddenly her heart was in her throat. Flirtatious glances from Jeremy's busy dark eyes and Rachel's flippant remarks regarding him loomed in her thoughts. No, no. It was too ridiculous to even consider.

"I...I don't believe it," she said, shaking her head in wonder, yet beginning to examine it more carefully. "Where did you come up with all of this nonsense? Rachel is just recently divorced from a man named Troy Givens. I think you have the wrong person, Nigel, I really do. She and I met Jeremy Andrews for the first time yesterday while we waited for the tide to uncover the causeway." She pondered it for a moment then shook her head. "How do you explain Sara Danes then?"

"We think she was brought along to make it all look right. And no, I don't have the wrong person. Hampton has double checked. Think about it, Julia. What better job could Rachel have than gemologist? It gives her every opportunity to judge the value of family collections and set up heists to clear them out. If you'll cool your heels a little, we'll try to decide what to do about it." He tucked in his shirt and tried to straighten his collar.

Julia felt as if she had been dumped in the ocean without a life raft. Nigel deliberately clouded her thoughts with doubts to get her to stay and listen. She could see it in his face. Reluctantly she went back to the parlor and sat down by the fire, her brain rambling in confusion.

"How did you become acquainted with Rachel?" he asked.

Julia told him about everything leading up to the trip.

"Don't you trust me to be fair about the jewels?" he asked, as though his heart was breaking because she apparently hadn't trusted him from the beginning. He shrugged with dismay.

"Perhaps I should be asking the same question, but I'll answer yours if I must. Of course I trust you," she said with a voice entirely too sweet.

"What reason would I have to distrust a person who has, so far, shown himself only capable of lies? I came to Gorlachen to help with all those things you mentioned in that warm inviting letter--with ownership of gems among them. Well, it so happens I wouldn't know a real emerald from a wine-bottle chip. I mean, you've lived with all this wealth." She threw her arms about in an exaggerated wave over the room. "We don't live this way in the States."

"I think I understand," he said. He deliberately took his time poking up the fire, as though grasping for a way to get through to her. "What do you think Rachel wants from the trip?"

"She was planning to look at the jewelry with me. She loves antique pieces and is an expert at placing a value on them. Besides that, she's having a wonderful time. I think...."

"You think what?"

"I was going to say that she seems to enjoy Jeremy Andrews, but now you tell me they're married...." Again confusion overcame her and she couldn't finish what she was about to say.

Nigel waited patiently while he considered her words. "Did it ever occur to you that the kind of valuable historical jewelry we're talking about might be in a safe place somewhere other than the castle? That outsiders would never be allowed to lay eyes on the real pieces except for very rare and special occasions?"

Julia sat statue-like on the edge of her chair and watched the fire shower sparks intermittently over the blazing interior of the fireplace. She felt so delicately brittle that if someone touched her she might shatter into a zillion pieces. She studied him thoughtfully. What a difference there was between the way she and Nigel were raised, even though they were of the same bloodline.

"If that's the case, I'm not sure I'm the proper person to own them," she said quietly.

"I knew the moment I laid eyes on you that you were a Maltby. Never forget that, Julia. And remember that the importance of the jewels has nothing whatever to do with their monetary value. It has to do with history, with all that has gone before. You and I are only the custodians of that history, keeping the ancient pieces safe for the continuum of past to present to future. The generations have done it before us, now it's our turn."

He spoke with such passion Julia was mesmerized. She found herself becoming more and more impressed with the intensity with which her cousin carried out his lordship. She massaged her forehead, trying to relax and absorb what seemed to be a great responsibility on her part that she was not quite sure she fully understood.

"What do you want from me?" she asked cautiously.

Nigel stood up and began to pace the floor with his back to her. Then, abruptly, he turned and stopped directly in front of her, nearly walking on her toes. "I want a partner to help me make decisions. I have no one." His blue-gray eyes were very clear and penetrating.

"But you own the castle and grounds," Julia said. "I know little about it. If I could be helpful perhaps I wouldn't need this dramatic lecture."

"It's true, I own the castle, but you own the house I live in and the acreage surrounding it."

Julia examined the room, admiring the warm charm of the old manor house. "I'm taking your word for that. My father never once mentioned it to me."

"Like the castle dining room?"

"Exactly."

"Your father was a very bitter man, my dear. He had detested my father all his life because the older brother inherits the property and the title that goes with it. There was nothing my father could do about that. After grandfather died, my father and grandmother decided to turn over to your father the one piece of property that was closest to their hearts, Dunrose Manor. He didn't seem to hold it in very high regard, however. Grandmother used to write to him and ask for advice about the upkeep of the place, but your father never once expressed an opinion about it. I finally took the house over myself to save it."

He sat down opposite Julia and watched her skeptically, as though wondering if he had said all the wrong things and she might suddenly dissolve and leave him alone again.

Julia was unable to move. Was that why her father had talked about the castle and his life in it only in terms of momentous historical facts?

Had he loved it so intensely he could not bear to have it go to his older brother? She found it difficult to believe. It was not her father's style.

"You'll have to understand that my father became thoroughly Americanized," she laughed, hoping to ease the tension between them. "He was a highly stylized actor. He and my mother were saturated with the theater. After father became involved with Broadway I'm not sure he gave much further thought to medieval castles and manor houses in Northumberland. You'll have to admit this life you live is highly unusual. Not everyone is suited to it, I think. I suspect that was true of my father."

She stopped talking when she saw Nigel's eyes glued to her face. He heard something. A circular gesture with his hand encouraged her to continue talking while he motioned toward the upstairs with the other hand. What did he hear?

Julia peered cautiously into the upper reaches of the stairwell. Then she heard it. Somewhere over their heads the floor creaked several times under stealthy footsteps.

"My mother was better known as my father's wife than she was for her actual acting ability. Father was always very careful to include her prominently in public and private matters having to do with his career," she said, bewildered, while she watched Nigel pick up a heavy silver candelabra from the sideboard near the bottom of the stairwell, then stalk without a sound to the landing while he motioned again with his hand for her to continue talking.

She continued to rattle on, quoting her mother and father on a range of mundane subjects while Nigel skulked silently to the top of the steps. Light from the landing window glinted menacingly from the silver piece he carried. Julia stopped talking and held her breath.

There were no further sounds. Someone heard what they wanted to hear and probably escaped the same way they came in.

Nigel rushed down the steps and into the kitchen where he spoke on the telephone to security people. "Search Dunrose Manor immediately. Stop any guests or unidentified persons on the grounds." Within minutes the house was crawling with uniformed security people.

Paul Hampton, wearing heavy yellow rain gear, burst into the parlor, and when he saw Julia he stopped so suddenly he nearly tripped over his own feet. "So here you are. What in bloody hell? I've been looking for you all morning," he said coldly while trying to catch his breath.

"Forget it, Paul," Nigel said. "Julia knows you're Paul Hampton."

"Thank God for that," Hampton said. He mopped his brow as though Julia was more of a burden than he cared to deal with. "This whole bloody thing has turned into a pot boiler."

"What's happened now?" Nigel said.

"All the guests were accounted for but Julia and Rachel Givens. The others are in the castle library playing medieval games. Now I've found Julia, but where is Rachel Givens, that's what I'd like to know. She's deliberately sneaked off somewhere against the rules." He looked at Julia with reproach. "Here I'm supposed to be keeping an eye on you, young lady, and half the time I can't even find you."

"You're keeping an eye on me?" she said with dismay.

"It so happens it's my job. There's been a murder since you arrived here, remember? We'd like to figure out who did it before it happens again. A little cooperation, like reporting when you're leaving the castle, would be *most* appreciated."

"You may call me Miss Maltby, if you don't mind. I thought Inspector Walpole was in charge...."

"Good grief," Nigel interrupted, "I'm beginning to see it's not a good idea to leave the two of you alone to rag each other. If this keeps up I'll have to hire a referee too. Please, let's put our differences aside for now."

Hampton started to say something, then clearly thought better of it and gave Julia a severe look instead.

She smiled sweetly. Her composure was only a facade, however. The idea that he might identify the buckle found in the sculpture gallery this morning left her insides trembling. And what about the film container? There was no reasonable way to explain how it came to be in her shoe. She could not possibly tell Hampton about it without appearing to be a murder suspect.

Chapter 12

Nigel and Paul Hampton went off with security people, so Julia walked slowly back to the castle alone, her thoughts churning over the outrageous information Nigel gave her about Rachel and Jeremy Andrews. None of it was solved for her when she saw Rachel coming down the path toward her.

"Did you go to Dunrose Manor without me? Damn it, Julia. I wanted to see it in the worst way. *Damn* it." She stamped her foot for emphasis and looked with longing toward the manor house. "What's it like?"

"Very English," Julia said coldly, looking at Rachel as though she were a snake ready to strike. She had no idea what to think after what Nigel told her. "Why are you so interested in it?"

"I thought it was one of the things we came to see. Have you forgotten how excited you were the day you called and invited me along? 'We're going to see a real English Manor house, Rachel,' you said." She slipped her arm through Julia's. "Honey, I'm sorry things have not worked out well with you and your cousin. I know it's a bitter disappointment for you, but I do hope you won't blame me."

"Did I say I was blaming you?" Julia answered almost too quickly. "Maybe you should go find Jeremy Andrews and see what he thinks about it."

Puzzled, Rachel dropped Julia's arm and faced her. "Maybe you'd care to explain that remark. Granted, I find Jeremy Andrews interesting, but what does that have to do with you and me?"

Julia could have bitten her tongue. "I...I only meant that the two of you seem to be getting on well. I guess I'm a little jealous of your time, that's all."

"Jealous of my time? I'd be happy to spend more time with you if I could ever find you. Now, promise me you'll take me to visit Dunrose Manor before we leave and I'll forgive you." They laughed and linked arms.

"It's a promise," Julia said.

They walked arm in arm through the garden with Rachel babbling about the glowing health of English perennials, while Julia wondered what reasonable explanation she could give Rachel for not allowing her to see the antique jewelry. And had Rachel really not seen Dunrose Manor? Here she was out walking the grounds alone, and she seemed to know where Julia had been. Did she follow her to Dunrose Manor and listen to her conversation with Nigel from an upstairs listening post? She could have arrived there before Julia did and waited in one of the many rooms.

"What have you been doing this morning?" Julia asked timidly. "I understood there were to be medieval games for the guests in the library."

"I hate macho pissing games," Rachel said with a sneer. "They bore me to death. I decided to go upstairs and milk the bathroom faucet for every drop of warm water to rinse out undies. From the looks of this sky, they'll still be dripping when we're ready to leave here."

"Oh, I say. One moment please," came a shout from behind them.

Rachel stopped and waited for a uniformed security man to approach. His straight blond hair bobbed up and down with each brisk step. When he was close enough to recognize Julia, his businesslike countenance turned to a smile.

"Good morning, Miss Maltby." He eyed Rachel. "The two of you have been together all morning, have you?"

"Yes, we have," Julia said with a tone of dismissal. She took Rachel's arm and pulled her along.

"Well...sorry to bother," he said, appearing reluctant to let them go. No doubt he was ordered to check out Rachel, but Julia was not about to allow it until she solved this nonsense for herself. She would not give Nigel further cause to accuse her friend.

The guard hurried on down the path, biting his lip as though he wished he could question them more thoroughly, but Julia knew he would not risk irritating a Maltby.

"What was that all about? You nearly pulled my arm out of the socket," Rachel said, and pulled her arm away.

"Who knows?" Julia's heart was beating double time. "They've probably had a prowler or something. This is such a big place to look after. With a murder to solve, they're being careful to check everyone who's out and about. And I don't want to give Nigel the pleasure of allowing one of his guards to detain us."

"I don't know what you're talking about," Rachel said, her face scrunched into a questioning frown.

"Just move on. Can't you see I need to put Nigel in his place?" Julia smarted. She didn't intend to turn against Rachel and throw her to the dogs unless there was positive proof she was a thief. All the same, she was glad to know Paul Hampton would be keeping an eye on all of them at the castle. She assumed he knew his job well, but she would have to go some to keep him in his place. She would not tolerate his ordering her about like a child. Abruptly a chill passed over her and she felt lonely and frightened. She must stay away from isolated places, stay near the group until this whole ugly business was cleared up.

"The plan is to visit Rochlund Abbey after lunch. You're going, aren't you, Julia?" Rachel asked in a simpering tone as though she were dealing with a mentally ill patient. They stopped at the door of Julia's room.

"Yes, of course," Julia said, forcing gaiety. "I want to see everything I possibly can while I'm here."

"Atta girl." Rachel gave Julia's arm a squeeze. "I knew you'd snap out of it."

Julia flinched slightly from Rachel's touch, disgusted with herself for doubting her. She just didn't know whom to believe. It was such a miserable way to treat a friend. If Nigel was planning to trap Rachel, Julia simply would not be a party to it.

Chapter 13

The minute Rachel disappeared from the corridor Julia set out to find a stairwell that led to the top of the keep. She must see where her father chose to live in this most unusual of places he called home. The portrait Nigel drew of him was not the one Julia held in her heart.

After circling through seemingly endless gray tunnels, she could find no evidence of a stairwell. She waited impatiently in her room, pacing the floor, while the noncommittal servant girl who answered her bell summoned the head maid.

Within minutes a prim uniformed woman with a smooth ageless face and worried hazel eyes stood before Julia. Julia had never seen her before. "Yes, mum?"

"What level of the keep am I on?"

"Level three, mum."

"How many levels are there?"

"Five in all," the woman said curtly, sizing her up for trouble. "Neither four nor five is open to guests."

"Is there a stairwell?" Julia met a stern level gaze. She was obviously dealing with the woman responsible for keeping curious bed and breakfast guests at bay.

"Only Lord Maltby can allow guests above the third level. He is not available at the moment, mum."

"I'm Julia Maltby," she said directly, getting a savory heady taste of the power of the name. "Would you direct me to the stairwell please?"

The woman looked her over, as though trying to decide whether or not she should take orders from her. Finally, satisfied that Julia would behave responsibly if allowed to roam the place, she turned and started down the hall.

"Follow me, mum," she said.

They went at a brisk pace to the end of the corridor where the woman stopped and pulled a long thin key from a jacket pocket and inserted it into a tiny hole in a stone in the wall. A very narrow wooden door, paved on the hall side with artificial stone, opened onto a stone stairwell cut into the wall's thickness.

Julia shook her head in wonder. The place was full of gimmicks and camouflage. A musty odor of disuse brought to reality how many years had gone by since her father set foot in the castle. Suddenly it all seemed so sad. Had her father really been as unhappy here as Nigel claimed? She climbed steep dark stairs, crossed the landing on the fourth level, then climbed again.

The stairs led into a great hall. The roof was not as high, nor the room as large as the hall downstairs, but it was a very elegant room with a stylish molded plaster ceiling. Heavy dark blue draperies blotted the light from several small windows to prevent damage to blue silk-hung walls and a number of early Italian tapestries, while white canvas throws protected dark mountainous humps of stuffed furniture. Julia gaped at fine Meissen porcelain pieces placed at random on dusty table tops. Blue and gold shown brightly from a medallion on a heavy dark blue oriental rug covered with clear plastic.

Julia gawked foolishly at the room's opulence. Her brain insisted on projecting an overlay of a small New York apartment with novel modern furnishings. Why did her father want to change his life so drastically when he moved to the States? What was he trying to get away from?

She wandered through high French doors into the bedroom. Here it was quite another story, like a different universe. The oak furnishings were modern. Pale yellow walls were papered with provocative photographs of a beautiful young woman with curly brown hair and cheerful bright blue eyes enhanced with lavish makeup. The photographs had been cut from film-star magazines, billboards, and advertisements of one kind or another.

Julia studied the woman in wonder. After she thought about it for a time the photographs were not too surprising. Her father loved the theater. As a youth he obviously had a great admiration for this beautiful young film star. She chuckled when she remembered how, at the age of twelve, she was hopelessly in love with Robert Redford. She plastered his photographs all around her room in a clever pattern of overlays and unusual arrangements, much like these photographs that were posted around her father's bedroom. Like father, like daughter?

Subconsciously, Julia heard the swish, swish of footsteps on the stone stairs, but she was so intent upon her own emotions that she paid no attention to them. She knew who it was anyway.

"No one gets away with anything around here, do they?" she asked without turning.

"I hope not. I count on Mrs. Winston to run a tight ship for me." Nigel came up beside her, and together they studied the photographs.

Julia noticed he had changed to a jade green outfit after their rather tedious bout earlier. The color was reflected in his eyes, or did he wear contact lenses to match his outfits? He smelled of soap and scented lotion. Apparently he was a man who did not tolerate untidiness for long.

"I knew the minute I spoke of it you'd come here straightaway. I'd have brought you myself if I hadn't been tangled up with security."

"Who is she?" Julia asked, indicating the photos with a movement of her head.

"My mother," he said casually. "A beauty, eh?"

Julia jerked her eyes to his. "This woman is your mother? But why are all of these photographs of her...." Julia felt his discomfort as he watched the pain of the revelation rise to shadow her eyes like a protective medieval shield.

"Don't be naive, Julia. Have you never heard of two men in love with the same woman?"

"Well...yes, but...." She gazed around her. Suddenly everything about the room suggested intimacy and spent passion.

75

"Your father moved to New York to get away from the place when he discovered it was his brother she really loved. I supposed you knew it."

"You didn't tell me the full truth earlier today then, did you, about his loathing the tradition of the oldest son inheriting?"

"Look, don't be upset, Julia. It's all a piece of the same cloth."

"But my father loved my mother deeply. They had a happy merry-go-round kind of life together on the stage. He showered gifts and love on both of us," She gawked foolishly at the photographs and tried to fit her father in around them.

"Well, there you have it," he said, but his smile was tight and unconvincing. "He fell in love with another woman. These photographs are nothing but remnants of the past. What young man has not been in love several times before he marries, eh, Julia?"

"Then why are they still here?" she persisted, looking at them doubtfully. A numbness crept around her heart leaving her voice to ring throughout a hollow body. She waved her arms over the room. "Why are they still here wrapped around these draped ghosts of my father's past?"

Abruptly Nigel began to laugh. He took Julia by the shoulders and turned her to face him.

"Stop and think about it, my dear. Your father has been gone a long time. I have been trying patiently to teach you that historical castles are places where things are not changed merely on a whim. We owe it to history, do we not? My father left the photographs here on purpose. When I was old enough to understand, he brought me here one day on the pretext of taking them down. I think what he really wanted was to find a place where he was highly motivated to talk to me about sex.

"He chose the right spot. He told me the whole story in a very graphic way with picture books and educational diagrams. All he had to do was gaze at these pictures of his wife when she was young and beautiful and he was off again on some different aspect of man's relationship with woman, pitfalls and all. I remember thinking what a nasty business sex sounded and how I would certainly never become involved in it." He laughed heartily, as though he was well versed in sexual techniques that dramatically dwarfed his father's efforts.

"Anyway, by the time he was finished, he decided the photographs were such a thorough historical record of my mother's career on the stage that he left them where they are. And that's that. While they may not mean much to you, they mean a great deal to *me*." He put an arm around Julia and gave her a hug while he laughed heartily. "Besides, my dear Julia, just think of it. Wouldn't it have been too bad if we had turned out to be brother and sister?"

Julia was not amused. She frowned at him, deep in thought. "What happened to her? Your mother, I mean."

"She gave up her stage career to marry my father. They had an off-again on-again time of it. She died three years ago, to spite my father I think."

"I'm sorry," Julia murmured.

"No need to be. Your family was not treated well at her hands. She always resented it that your father and his cousin married and continued with their careers in the theater, while she had to give up hers. She never allowed me to write, and forbade both my father and me to send photographs. She always feared she would look too old to her former lover. Actually, she needn't have worried. She was still quite beautiful the day she died."

Julia could see that the conversation was painful for him. He looked away while he talked. "It used to break my heart when I looked at your picture and realized I couldn't invite you here. In spite of it I loved my mother deeply. She was a dazzling light in this dark castle. I shall always miss her."

"Yes, I'm sure," Julia said lamely. His mother sounded like a very complicated woman. Julia was glad she was not *her* mother. Did she ever truly have a chance to be a woman in her own right, or was she married to an ancient castle and its continuum of history?

"It's hard to understand why you'd follow such childish rules your mother insisted on," Julia said, trying to keep up her end of the conversation. "You wanted us to be a family, but how could that happen when these photographs were still hanging in my father's bedroom to remind everyone of the past? If your mother feared she'd look old in a photograph, she must have still had feelings for my father. Why else would she care what he thought?"

77

Tears of dismay and sorrow stung Julia's eyes. She closed them so she could no longer see the pictures. "Please have these photographs removed at once. No wonder my father never wanted to come back to his home." Julia could not bear the thought that her father had loved this woman, been rejected by her, then married an available cousin, her mother, as a second choice.

Nigel stood perfectly still, his face flushed with quick anger. Julia's eyes widened to see his fist double into a tight knot. This cousin of hers was used to giving orders, not taking them.

"May I remind you that these photographs don't belong to you? In spite of your father, they will not be removed from this room. You're right, you know. At one time I hoped we might be a family, but I can see now that it isn't going to be possible." He turned sharply and strode across the bedroom and through the great room.

His remark served to widen the rift between them and reminded Julia that *she* owned Dunrose Manor. She thought she would never have a use for it, but after seeing it...well...she finally fell in love, didn't she? With a fifteenth-century manor house? She must do something about solidifying her ownership of it before she left for the States. Perhaps somehow, someday, she'd find a way to come back and live in it.

"By the way," she called after him, "did security find anyone lurking about Dunrose Manor this morning?"

"No, they found nothing. Do be careful wandering about the castle alone, Julia. I'll find Paul Hampton before lunch and see to it you're looked after at the abbey. We don't need any more trouble. And be sure to close the hall door on level three. I don't want tourists up here." He clattered down the steps, slamming the door at the bottom.

Julia wanted to be away from arguments. She left the bedroom and ambled through the other rooms of her father's apartment--another bedroom with sparse furnishings, and a tiny, poorly-equipped kitchen.

In the back hallway, between the kitchen and bathroom, she stopped abruptly. In front of her set a small walnut bookshelf with a hand-carved shell at the top. It matched the one her father used in his bathroom in their apartment in New York. He must have moved its mate with him when he left the castle. Suddenly she felt her father's presence and tears clouded her vision. It was the only thing in these lofty living quarters that even vaguely reminded her of him, except for Nigel's looks and speech habits. How could her father have lived such a happy and thoroughly modern American life if he really longed for the love of a woman who lived in a medieval castle in the northernmost part of England?

She closed off the ornate rooms and walked quickly down the steep steps. There was no way she could answer the question. Her father obviously made a choice and stuck with it. He chose Broadway and her mother. Suddenly she felt quite sure his time was not spent mooning over medieval dining rooms, manor houses, or his brother's wife. She must see to it that the photographs were removed from his bedroom to end the matter once and for all, in spite of what Nigel thought. They didn't belong there.

Chapter 14

Quiet reigned throughout the castle. Julia was not sure whether it was because the inhabitants were mourning the loss of Professor Quayle, or more likely, that they were petrified at the thought of murder and kept to their rooms for safety's sake.

She climbed onto her grandmother's great bed and lay with her hands across her middle like a stone effigy, staring without sight at the room around her. How did she ever embrace the ridiculous notion that she and Nigel Maltby might fall in love? What kind of naive fairy-tale nonsense was she entertaining?

A narrow shaft of lemon sunshine fell across the bed. She wondered if perhaps it was an omen of better times ahead. Scattered thoughts of branding irons, sculpted busts, flirting brown eyes, and flying shoe buckles reeled through her brain. She was on the brink of sleep when the welcome silence was shattered by a brisk knock on the door.

"Who is it?" she asked, not wanting to see anyone.

"Inspector Walpole here."

"I'm resting," Julia said, She had a tension headache. Perhaps he would come back later.

"Open the door, please, Miss Maltby. I must ask you a few questions."

Julia sat up and tried to massage away the pain that throbbed relentlessly through her head. Detectives were all alike. They were impatient and even said the same rude things to women through closed doors. Besides, it irritated her the way he smelled so strongly of rain and damp wool, as though there were a wet dog in the room. She jerked the door open and turned back to a chair by the cold fireplace. She dropped onto it and gave him a decidedly unfriendly look.

"Sorry to bother like this, Miss Maltby. It's all a matter of formalities you understand," he wheezed.

"Get on with it," she said impatiently. "I have a splitting headache."

He ignored her plea as though every woman he interviewed about murder complained of a headache and he learned to expect it. He sat down while he dawdled over filling his pipe. Before he lit it he waved it toward her for an okay. When she only shrugged, he lit it, then leveled his eyes on hers. Now that he had gained entrance to her room he seemed to be in no particular hurry. He zipped a plaid tobacco pouch shut and stored it in his breast pocket.

"What were you doing in the sculpture gallery around ten o'clock last night, Miss Maltby?"

Julia's mouth flew open like the miniature door of a cuckoo clock.

"Who on earth told you I was in the gallery?"

He smiled like she was a very poor actress. "We all have our work to do, do we not?" He reached into the pocket of his worn tweed jacket and pulled out a shiny object. "I believe this buckle fits one of your shoes."

The crepe-soled canvas shoes with one buckle missing were in plain sight under the end of the mahogany bed. There was no point in denying it. Why was she not at least deceptive enough to keep them out of sight?

"What if it is mine?" she said irritably. "Just because I was downstairs last night doesn't mean I murdered the professor, if that's what you're getting at. I happen to know there were several people downstairs against the rules last night."

Apparently Walpole did not consider it an adequate answer. He raised his eyebrows and shrugged. "We're talking about you, are we not? Mr. Churchill once said, 'If you meet trouble promptly without flinching, you reduce the problem by half.'" He fastened pale eyes on hers.

Julia stared into the black gaping hole of the unlit fireplace. He was right. The shortest way around the problem was the truth. Nigel and Paul Hampton would not allow him to badger her.

"I...." She threw up her hands in despair. "I don't even know where to begin it's all so absurd. I don't understand it myself."

"Let's start from the beginning then."

Before Julia had a chance to collect her thoughts, the door flew open and in huffed Nigel with Paul Hampton at his heels. The door banged shut with a deep rattling echo.

"Julia, why in bloody hell didn't you tell me you were in the sculpture gallery last night?" Nigel hissed through clenched teeth, as though he had not quite pried them apart after their quarrel earlier in the day. "Paul just reported that the buckle found near Quayle's body came from your shoe. Are you trying to make a fool of me? Just what do you know about Professor Quayle's murder?" His face was molten with fury.

Paul Hampton stood with his legs apart, leaning forward with a shame-on-you look, as though he expected a full confession of murder on the spot.

The room was suddenly hot and uncomfortable. Julia gazed helplessly at her three accusers. She could hardly breathe. She shifted her focus back to the fireplace. Obviously there was no room here for Mr. Churchill's truth. She would have to explain to Nigel about the sculpture gallery, but she was not going to confide in anyone about the mysterious roll of film. This afternoon she would leave the group at the abbey and find a place to have it developed. Was there something there for her eyes only?

"If you and I can talk alone, Nigel, I think I can explain." Her voice was plaintive, like a frightened little girl's, but she could not control it.

Nigel continued to glare at her for a moment, then motioned for the others to leave. "Well?" he snapped. "Get on with it."

Julia started at the beginning and went through all of her emotions and actions since she arrived at Castle Gorlachen. The longer she talked, the more angry she became with the situation in which she felt he placed her.

"This is really your fault, you know, for trying to hide your identity. Otherwise I would have no need to comb this castle in the dark for the branding iron. You may be Lord of Gorlachen, whatever that means to you, but let me tell you that it doesn't make a tinker's damn worth of difference to me," she finished wrathfully.

Nigel sank into the depths of a chair and wheezed a heavy sigh as though she had hit him in the chest with a fist. "This scares me, Julia. You said a security man called out through the gallery. That would be highly unlikely. The sculpture gallery has been closed to the public since grandmother died some fifteen years ago. I don't keep security people down there." He seemed almost on the verge of tears. "Gorlachen has her own internal security. There isn't one person in a million who would venture into this mammoth castle alone in the dark. I don't even do it myself anymore, and it's as familiar to me as the back of my hand."

"The mystery security man and I were not the only two down there last night," Julia said solemnly.

Nigel frowned. He looked so tragic Julia actually began to enjoy herself. "Whoever was in the gallery followed me all the way. I feel sure of it. There was a faint metallic tink that stopped every time I stopped. I thought at first the sound was made somehow by my flashlight, but I tested it as I walked along, and I know that wasn't it."

"Could it have been one of the Eldreds? They seem to be the ones who prowl about in the dark," he said, shrugging as though there was little he could do about it. Julia could tell by the lost look on his face he knew it was a long shot.

"I can't imagine the Eldreds involved in a murder, but you never really know people, do you? They both worked in the Dutch underground during the war. Maybe they're more experienced at covering their tracks than we know," Julia suggested. Did Mae lie to her about leaving the jacket in the dining room? And there was the tiff between John and the professor at dinner....

"Bloody hell," Nigel lamented. "Everybody in the bloody place was down there for one reason or another last night. Jeremy Andrews and Sara Danes were scouting for aspirin. According to them Sara drank too much wine at dinner and had a miserable headache. Mae was after her jacket, and John Eldred was blasting about, looking for her...or someone he could cuddle up to." He frowned like he'd just bitten into a sour apple. "A lot of good it does to make rules."

"I don't know who followed me and I'm not sure I want to know. When I got back to this room there was a fire going in the fireplace. I thought all along that *you*, or perhaps Paul Hampton, lit it for me. But I should have known it was too much to ask," she said haughtily. "Anyway, I didn't build it. I think someone waited here for me while I was downstairs, but had to leave before I returned."

"But who would that have been, and why?"

"I don't know," Julia said softly. "I really don't know."

It wasn't quite the truth. Because of the argument about the cameras, she knew it must have been Professor Quayle. He surely photographed something that caused him to suddenly hide the film container in her shoe, then leave. Why was he hiding in her room? Did Mae hear him being dragged away from Julia's room to be murdered? She shuddered and clamped her teeth together to stop their chattering.

Julia and Nigel sat quite still, looking at each other skeptically, as though trying to decide whether they could fully trust each other. At last Nigel got up and crossed to the door.

"I'll speak to Walpole, tell him your story. I don't know if he'll accept it from me, but maybe he won't bother you anymore today so you can enjoy your trip to the abbey. Enjoy it fully, Julia. The abbey is such a heartrending meeting with ghosts of the past."

Julia watched him hurry down the hall. More historical passion, but ghosts of the past? She had already encountered more ghosts of the past than she cared to deal with.

When Nigel disappeared from view, Julia opened the hall door to her father's apartment. She didn't lock it this morning in case she wanted to return. She scurried up the steps. She must remove the photographs while there was still time, before they were called to lunch.

A sharp scraping on the floor, accompanied by other sounds of a human presence, reached her before she hit the top step. She stopped and listened, then stepped quietly through the great room and peered through the bedroom door.

A handsome blond, blue-eyed young man in green coveralls was perched precariously on a high ladder placed against the wall.

"What are you doing here?" Julia asked.

The young man jumped at the sound of her voice and scrambled to catch himself before he fell off the ladder. "Jeez," he said sharply, "why don't you make yourself known? There's been a murder here, ya know."

"Sorry," Julia said.

"Lord Maltby told me to take these photos down," he said, unable to tear his eyes from the photo of the actress's cleavage. "Whew," he said under his breath.

Julia didn't expect Nigel to order the pictures taken down, and yet he did it immediately, and for her. Her conscience troubled her. She studied the photographs, trying to be objective. They were part of Gorlachen's historical continuity, that was true. Perhaps she was too hasty in her insensitive rejection of them.

"Leave them," she heard herself say abruptly. "I'll see to them myself."

He pulled his eyes away from the photographs and looked her over appreciatively.

"That sounds good to me, luv, but Lord Maltby...."

"I said it's all right. I'm Julia Maltby. I'll see to it."

"Yes, ma'am. If you say so." He quickly pulled down the ladder and banged noisily through the great room and down the steps with it, as though glad to distance himself from what might have been the loss of his job had he carried his flirtation further.

Julia followed to the lower hall. She would not come here again. Nigel was right. It was all in the past and had nothing to do with their lives now. She wanted to go directly to her room and ring for a maid to lock the stairwell, but she was snagged by the sight of the professor's body being loaded into the hearse.

Chapter 15

"Isn't it exciting?" Rachel said with delight as she climbed into the van and took a seat beside Julia.

Julia jumped from raw nerves. "Isn't what exciting?"

"Everything. The murder, the seedy inspector, the marvelous food, country manor houses, and now an eleventh-century abbey. It's absolutely thrilling!" She took up an exuberant conversation on the history of Rochlund Abbey with Annalisa and Nigel, who sat across the aisle from them.

Julia was still shaken from watching Professor Quayle's body being removed from the castle. She was walking through the hall on her way back to her room when her eye was caught by a movement as she glanced down the arrow slit. Until she saw the body bag, nothing about the demise of the professor bothered her. Now she was shaken by a sudden apprehension of evil.

Her hand went to the pocket of her denim jacket where she stored the film until she could figure out what to do with it. She feared she might lose it. But it was still there where she put it for safe keeping before she left her room, but so far things were not going the way she hoped. She thought they would all drive their own cars. Then she could leave the group and see to the developing of the film. Now she had to find some other way to have it developed. What on earth could she do about it now? She glanced behind her.

Paul Hampton was not in the van. He came along later in an extra car that brought the servants with drinking water and snacks. According to Nigel, Hampton was going to keep an eye on all of them at the abbey. Apparently someone in this group murdered Professor Quayle. The thought was shocking.

Julia glanced sharply at Rachel. She was a tall, slender, very pretty woman in her early thirties with dark almond-shaped eyes and clear translucent skin. What possible interest could she have in Professor Quayle that would make her a murder suspect? Julia's thoughts were chaotic. She looked away when Rachel's eyes met hers. It was difficult to be friends with someone who lied to you. And wasn't Rachel overacting just a bit about the marvels of all these medieval things they were seeing and eating?

Jeremy sat in the back seat with his arm around Sara Danes. Their heads were together, engaged in intimate conversation. If he was married to Rachel, wasn't he going a little overboard in his role of playing up to Sara Danes? What must Rachel think?

The ruins of Rochlund Abbey loomed against the lush green hillside like a storm-battered ship gone aground. Pearly gray stones jutted into the air in spikes, pillars, and cubicles, leaving only vague suggestions of former grandeur. Unearthed stone foundations formed geometric patterns that snaked in and out of existing walls.

Rachel got out of the van first and struck out across a well-manicured lawn. "Come on, Julia," she said, "this is an incredible spot. Maybe we'll discover something no one else has seen."

"Let's wait for the others." Julia wanted to share Rachel's enthusiasm, but instead she lagged behind with two servants who lugged along a large picnic basket filled with the trappings for tea later in the afternoon. She waited for Paul Hampton to catch up. He was supposed to be a long-lost cousin. They could reasonably pay some attention to each other without causing speculation among the others.

Hampton strolled casually with his hands in the pockets of a pair of olive drab combat fatigues. A baggy cotton T-shirt said "Laugh a Lot." He visited amiably with John and Mae Eldred paying no attention to Julia.

Julia watched Nigel get out of the van and wait patiently for Annalisa to gather up a straw hat, suntan lotion, a pair of red sneakers, and other paraphernalia. Her black hair glinted with healthy purple highlights. The cotton-print long skirt she wore seemed too formal for the occasion. She was a full-bodied girl, somewhat older than Nigel, Julia guessed--interesting in her own dark way, but rather coarse. She didn't seem like the type to become First Lady of Gorlachen. Julia wondered if she and Nigel were lovers. Somehow she couldn't imagine it. She tried to conjure a picture of their bodies writhing in unison, but the image wouldn't come. She watched as they got Annalisa's belongings stowed in pockets and bags and fell in behind the rest of the group.

Nigel burst into laughter at something Annalisa said. A twinge of regret at her failed relationship with Nigel made Julia turn away from them to where weather-worn high jutting walls curved around the cloister. She was not in a festive mood anyway and saw no reason to pretend she was. She wished this silly charade would end so she could spend time with Nigel to settle things about Dunrose Manor, The National Trust, and the jewelry. They were the only real interests left to her at Gorlachen. She was so frustrated over how little time there was, only three full days left, that she completely forgot to be frightened of Inspector Walpole over his knowledge of her shoe buckle, or worry about developing the film.

The sweet heady odor of freshly-cut grass lured her to a wall where swollen clumps of lavender aubrietia cascaded in a charming display. She sat down on the grass and leaned drowsily against the wall to soak up the sun's warmth, listening to the voices on the other side as the explorers exclaimed over their ancient discoveries.

Abruptly Julia was aware of voices inside the cloister from two who fell some distance behind the others. As they approached the wall opposite her she heard Jeremy Andrews's voice. He sounded put out, but was in control of his emotions.

"Why would you think that, Sara? Now please don't cry. It meant nothing."

Sara Danes answered, her voice full of perplexity and hurt. "If you're going to flirt outrageously with every beautiful woman who comes along, then I'm through. I simply will not tolerate it."

"I told you, Rachel Givens means nothing to me. She was the one flirting with me, by the way, not the other way around. I hope you noticed that."

"You enjoyed it. Don't tell me you didn't."

"Let's not argue, Sara. We came to have a good time...."

As they moved away, Julia could no longer hear Sara's response. She sat perfectly still, too terrified to move. It sounded so easy for Jeremy to lie. Had he always been a liar? Julia wondered if she should find Paul Hampton to report the conversation. Instead, she let out a breath and leaned rigidly against the warm stone. There were so many things she needed to think about--whom she could or could not trust for one thing.

Doubts and uncertainties loomed large in her mind and seemed to reel and gyrate in some kind of nebulous speed-rigged galaxy of their own as she nodded off. Bodies--Rachel's, Nigel's, Jeremy's, Paul Hampton's, Mae's, John's?--without faces whipped frenetically through the arches like frightened children clinging to an amusement park ride. When Julia tried to approach, they disappeared, leaving only the clatter of machinery as they rode away.

She opened her eyes and realized she was dreaming. The clatter she heard was not amusement park machinery, but quick clackety-clack footsteps on the other side of the wall. A chilly wind had come up. It moaned and sighed eerily through the battered arches and broken tracery in the giant rose window.

She was not sure how long she slept. She jumped up. It must be time for tea.

She was starting to brush grass from her jeans when the heavy square stone crashed with a thunderous jolt squarely in the spot where she was sitting. Paralyzed, she gaped in awe as it bounced clumsily over the grass and finally settled on end against the wall. Retreating footsteps echoed through her head, but she could not tell from which direction they came.

She struggled to keep from panicking. In terror her eyes searched the top of the wall. A prominent dark hole near the base of a clump of aubrietia seemed to leer daringly at her. Someone tried to kill her.

It was the last straw. Fury engulfed her, and like the tentacles of a threatened octopus, squeezed all fear away. She stalked through the nearest arch to peer down the stone-paved cloister. There was no one in sight. If she could get her hands on whoever pushed that stone she would throttle him within an inch of his life. She ran to the open end of the walk that flowed away from the abbey and across a wide stretch of lawn bordered by thick deciduous woods. Mae and John Eldred walked stiffly across the grass and appeared to be angry with each other. Occasionally John tried to take Mae's hand, but she pushed it away and vigorously shook her head.

"Julia," John called when he saw her, "come murder a cup of tea with this gorgeous woman and me."

"Did you have to use that expression after all we've been through these last two days? Honestly, John, you're the world's most insensitive clod." Mae shook her head as though she was giving up on him completely and stomped out of sight amid the arches, leaving him to look after her in wonder.

Julia was too concerned with her own dilemma to care about theirs. She turned back to the walk and studied the spot where her unknown assailant climbed the wall to dislodge the stone. The wall was at least eight feet high and irregular enough to allow a toehold. Particles of flaked stone and bits of bruised aubrietia blooms littered the walk beneath the spot. She walked briskly through several arched passages toward the voices of the group. She held her breath. Was someone waiting for her in the shadows?

Abruptly, in a deeply shaded area near wide double arches where deep grass and wild flowers had been allowed to flourish, Julia caught her breath in a near scream when she stumbled over Jeremy Andrews and Sara Danes. They were entwined in a passionate embrace. Sara's skirt was twisted around her hips, and dark purple lipstick lay in a long smear across her face. Jeremy's trousers were loosened at the waist. Julia was so shocked at their behavior that she stood rigidly and stared open mouthed at them.

"Sorry," Jeremy stammered, and quickly hid their bodies beneath

Sara's printed full skirt, his face scarlet. Sara sat up, her look full of resentment at the invasion of privacy.

"I'm sorry...I didn't...."

Julia recovered her dignity, tried to act like she didn't see them, and excused herself. The argument behind the wall obviously was settled to the satisfaction of both. Julia hurried off, wishing she might never lay eyes on the cheating Jeremy Andrews again. It was disgusting that no one could be trusted anymore.

She found the other guests lounging on the grass near an ancient font converted to a temporary tea table. The ubiquitous white tablecloth and a rangy bouquet of aubrietia and mammoth golden dandelion blooms formalized the occasion. Would the English ever be broken of formalizing the least formal goings-on?

Paul Hampton leaned lazily against a rock wall holding forth on a news release about the recently discovered remains of the Spanish Armada off the island's northern tip. The whole group was caught up in the recitation complete with dates, causes, and number of ships involved. The English were up to their eyebrows in historical data it seemed. It was all well and good, but why had Hampton not been keeping an eye on her?

"Julia," Nigel whispered at her elbow. "I came looking for you a bit ago and found you sleeping peacefully against the wall. I didn't have the heart to waken you."

Julia studied his face. He was taunting her. Was he trying to kill her? How could she possibly confide in him now? It was Dunrose Manor he wanted, that was it. He brought her to Gorlachen to do away with her so he could keep Dunrose Manor. Everything fit. He hid his identity when she arrived. Then he insisted someone spied on them in the manor house to frighten her, but security found no one. He also knew the castle "like the back of his hand." He was the one who followed her through the endless castle rooms, making his way easily without a light, she was sure of it.

"What's wrong, Julia? You're looking at me so strangely. Has something happened?"

"No, no. I'm all right. I'm trying to wake up. I guess I was more tired than I realized. I didn't realize I slept so long." She tore her eyes away from his puzzled gaze and looked at her watch. "Here it is tea time."

Nigel looked at her oddly, then wandered off to consult with Paul Hampton. How easy it would be for him to pull the wool over Hampton's eyes, Julia thought. As Lord of Gorlachen he only needed to tell others what to do and they did it. If it were not for Walpole's orders to remain at Gorlachen she would leave for New York tomorrow. She must keep a very close eye on this cousin of hers.

A servant handed her a welcome cup of steaming tea and offered a selection of sandwiches and pastries from a rose-patterned china plate. Julia chose a tiny sandwich and some sort of tart with an oozing chocolate filling.

Rachel waved to her from where she sat with Annalisa on an oak garden bench. Her tea plate was loaded with goodies. She examined a chocolate morsel carefully, then popped it into her mouth.

"Mmmm. Delicious. Have a good nap?" she asked cheerfully.

"Very relaxing," Julia said, forcing a smile. Apparently all of the guests walked by and looked her over while she napped. She was just sitting down to enjoy her tea when she heard a car door latch behind her.

Inspector Walpole crossed the lawn toward them, trudging as heavily as his long reedy body would allow. He wore the same brown tweed jacket as though it were a professional badge to be reckoned with.

Relief rushed over Julia. She would tell him about the falling rock and he would do something immediately. She must also remember to tell him about the film. He walked directly to her.

"Miss Maltby? I must ask you to stay on the island for a few more days. This is normal procedure in a murder case, you understand." His eyes swept over her, then came back to gaze into hers with a sigh of regret, as though he decided she may well be the guilty one and he was terribly sorry for it.

Julia shook her head in disbelief. She wanted to laugh hysterically at the absurdities involved. She also wanted to plant a right uppercut on the tip of his pasty-skinned chin. Did he really think she came all this way from the States to murder a man in a medieval castle's sculpture gallery? And a man she barely knew at that? How terribly exotic of him. She didn't know exactly what he knew about her, but she learned a very interesting fact about him. The lawman was highly impractical. She would not tell him about the falling rock or the film. He wouldn't believe her anyway. She was going to have to solve this thing herself.

With no forethought at all, an idea struck her and there was no time to pause to consider its consequences.

"Well, Mr. Walpole, if that's the way things are, I have a little errand for you. I mean, I can't do errands if you're going to watch me every minute, can I?" she said brightly, turning what she hoped were wide innocent-looking eyes on his.

"And what might that be?" he asked skeptically as he took a step backward, as though he thought she might ask him to whip over to New York and pick up an extra change of clothes for her.

Julia moved ever so close to him and fluttered her long blond lashes as she spoke in a confidential whisper. "I have a roll of film here I'd like developed. It's photos I've taken of the castle and my new friends. No flashbulbs, of course. But you mustn't tell anyone. Mum's the word. I want it to be a surprise for the group's last evening together. You know, a little something fun to end the stay with?" She winked intimately while she fished in her jacket pocket for the film container. She laid it in his hand, allowing her fingers to linger on his a little longer than necessary.

Walpole jerked visibly at her touch, looked doubtfully at the container, then back at her. "This is highly irregular," he said, dropping his eyes under her direct gaze, "but I suppose in this instance I can manage it. For Lord Maltby's cousin. Yes, for you and Lord Maltby."

"Of course it's for Lord Maltby, but you won't tell him and ruin my little surprise, will you?" she murmured sweetly with her warm breath on his ear. "I'll expect to pay all the costs."

"There'll be no problem, Miss Maltby," he said stiffly, trying to keep his composure. He dropped the film container into a threadbare pocket and walked directly to Rachel.

There it goes. Julia could only hope Walpole would take her request seriously enough to get those pictures back to her pronto.

Walpole spoke to Rachel for several minutes while Rachel kept up a negative shake of the head as a puzzled frown gathered between her eyes, as though she could not quite believe what he was saying to her. It seemed like quite a monologue for a man who usually spoke in clipped sentences. Anger and dismay clouded Rachel's face. Julia figured he must be telling her that she, too, was to remain at Gorlachen.

Then Walpole took a deliberately paced trip across the lawn to Jeremy Andrews. It appeared that he, three, would have to stay on.

Julia could not hear what Jeremy told him, and from the grim set of his twisted angry mouth she was not sure she wanted to hear it. What about John and Mae Eldred? Was Walpole not going to insist they stay? Julia did not intend to count anybody out at this point.

Walpole appeared to have concluded his mission without making any demands on the Eldreds.

Julia sighed. Was she the one to be blamed for the murder? Or Rachel and Jeremy?

Chapter 16

Early evening sunshine bathed the abbey with a rich golden glow. Julia watched the arched shadows move swiftly across the lawn and pervade the ruins with the deep purple shades of approaching dusk. Lively scented wildflowers and damp earthiness mingled lightly in the air, lending a breath of life to a structure that had lost its usefulness four hundred years earlier.

"It's time to get back," Paul Hampton said from the top of a low stone wall. "There'll be plenty of time to rest and dress for dinner." He jumped down and strolled over to Julia. "Have a nice day, cuz?"

Julia could see he was enjoying not having to call her Miss Maltby in this situation. "Delightful. As far as the guests are concerned we're supposed to be loving cousins, so perhaps we should pay more attention to each other. Have you enjoyed the afternoon?" She slipped her arm through his. She hated to put out such nonsense, but it gave her a chance to stay near him for protection.

"It's too bad we have to be so closely related, isn't it?" His dark red-brown eyes, gazing suggestively into hers, appeared depthless in the shadows. "I'm as sorry as you are we haven't had more time together."

"That's what everyone here seems to be thinking about everyone else," she said drily and smiled to herself. One of the last things she wanted was a romance with a private English detective for fear he would turn out to be exactly like Inspector Walpole. Which reminded her, "What has been accomplished toward solving the murder of Professor

Quayle? Surely Walpole won't expect all of us to stay here for weeks. Are there any real suspects, or are we only playing cat and mouse?"

"That depends on who you ask," he said with a shrug.

"What do you mean?"

"No one is jolly well keen on being a murder suspect now, are they?"

She ignored his smugness. "Inspector Walpole says I must stay on at Gorlachen for a while. I suppose that means *I'm* a suspect."

"There you have it," he said seriously. "Looks like you brought trouble with you--Rachel and her husband, Andrews, eh? And you were in the sculpture gallery the night the professor was murdered, were you not? Cheeky of you, I must say, Julia, breaking the rules so blatantly-- and your shoe buckle found near the body and all. The Inspector found it himself. You haven't denied that it is your buckle, have you? What are the Inspector and I to think?"

She couldn't bear his smugness. "I have never denied being in the sculpture gallery, but I didn't kill Professor Quayle, for God's sake. I didn't even know he was downstairs while I was. And after all, I *am* a Maltby. I'm free to go anywhere or do anything I please in the castle. I seem to have to keep reminding you of that."

"Free to do anything you please, eh? Even to robbing your cousin's safe?"

"I don't...."

"Lord Maltby's safe in the castle office was robbed of several hundred pounds the same night Quayle died. Are you going to tell me you know nothing about that?"

"Absolutely nothing. This is the first I've heard of it." Her breath came hard and she felt slightly faint again. Did he think she was lying?

"I must say, you're a brave girl, Julia, having the courage to wander through that spooky old castle in the dark. Nigel toured me through it and told me about the scar on his arm. In fact, he showed me the irons you were supposedly looking for that night. We had a good laugh over our failure at switched identities. I guess we're not very good actors."

"That's the most accurate conclusion I've heard all day. The whole thing is so pointless I'm beginning to wonder what really lies behind it, and believe me, I intend to find out. And further, if you two want to laugh at me, why don't you just laugh in my face? I would appreciate it more--maybe even get a good laugh myself."

She was about to walk away from him, depressed at the thought that Nigel was telling Hampton every little thing she told him in confidence, when she decided she probably should give the detective a bit of new information while she had the chance.

"Oh, by the way. I stumbled over Jeremy Andrews and Sara Danes in the shadows of the arches--minus some of their clothes--a bit ago. I feel so sad that Rachel must put up with that jerk, no matter what her motives are."

"That's the kind of people we're dealing with here," Hampton frowned. "Why would Andrews do a thing like that? Now I suppose you've spoken to Rachel about it, eh? If the two of them begin battling we'll never catch them."

"Spoken to Rachel about it?" Julia cringed at the thought. Anger overwhelmed her and she wanted to slap him. "What do you take me for? If I knew Jeremy Andrews sleeps with every woman here I wouldn't tell Rachel. Besides, what is it you expect to catch them at, huh? Pinching jewelry of questionable value from your skinflint Lord of Gorlachen? Jewels that, quote, 'formerly belonged to the crown?' Well la-de-da," she sang cattily. "It would do my heart good if they got away with some of them. And as for the robbing of Nigel's safe, this is the first I've heard of it. Take it or leave it." She stomped off and left him to gaze awkwardly after her.

She turned to watch him jump into the white Land Rover with the other servants and drive off before the van Julia would ride in had a chance to leave. The other guests stared. What difference did it make what they thought of her anger? Julia flounced into the van and dropped into a seat beside Rachel.

"If your face were any longer you'd be a candidate for mortician, and I'd vote for you," Rachel said.

"Sorry." Julia leaned against the seat and closed weary eyes. "It's been a bit of a day."

"Quit pulling those understated British expressions on me, damn it. If you've had one hell of a day, why don't you say so. Mine's been no bed of roses either. I think Walpole actually believes I murdered Professor Quayle. Can you imagine that? I can't for the life of me think why he singled me out. There were several guests downstairs last night, any one of whom might have killed Quayle. I wasn't even among them, and yet, for some reason, I'm a suspect."

Rachel no more than finished her tirade when Julia heard Jeremy Andrews's voice from several rows behind her.

"Bloody bastard," came his disdainful voice. "How can I stay longer in Britain when I need to get back to work at the end of next week at the latest? I called the boss and told him I might be late getting back. I beat around the bush about why I needed a longer vacation. What was I supposed to say, that I'm a suspect in a murder case?"

Julia heard Sara murmuring words of consolation but she could not make them out.

Perhaps they did not understand how the inspector worked. He would begin by suspecting everyone, wouldn't he, then weed them out one by one? If Rachel and Jeremy were involved in jewelry heists and murder, let them pay for it. As for herself, Julia figured she knew now which button of Walpole's to push. A little flirting and personal attention accomplished her mission with the film. Yet, doing his job promptly was the thing that did him proud. She smiled at her success at fooling him. She fully expected him to show up at the door of her room in a couple of days with the photographs in hand, having guarded their secrecy with his life.

However, her good humor soon faded, for when she got back to the castle and entered her room, she immediately sensed that someone had been there before her. She halted for a moment, allowing her eyes to become accustomed to the late afternoon shadows. Yes, she was sure of it. But what was it, an aura, an odor, something out of place? She could not quite decide. She stepped inside the door and stood rigid, like a wooden soldier, while she studied the room.

A door of the armoire was ajar. She knew she had not left it open because she had always been very particular about closing doors that hid the clutter of life. She approached it timidly, like seeking out a land mine. Was there someone waiting inside to throttle her for some reason of which she was unaware?

She eased the door open. Several of her dresses had been pulled from their hangers and lay in a jumble at the bottom of the cabinet. It was the only visible evidence that the room had been very discreetly taken apart, and had, just as carefully, been put back together. Nothing was missing. What did she have that anyone else could possibly want? Her jewelry was nothing to shout about, and her clothes certainly were not couture. It left only one possibility. Someone was looking for that film. How far would they go to find it?

Chapter 17

Julia dressed carefully for dinner in a silver-gray satin cocktail dress that bared shapely freckled shoulders. Her hair stood in untamed spikes around her head--a style flashy enough to keep a high profile in the midst of the group for safety's sake. A shimmering lip gloss added a romantic touch. Might Nigel ignore his silly disguise and come to collect her for dinner? There were still those things they needed to talk about. She wanted to assure him he could live in Dunrose Manor for the rest of his days, and he could keep all of the family jewelry. All she wanted was her life.

When he didn't come, she tripped down the stairs alone, teetering across the dining room's uneven stone floor in backless silver heels. A rope of floppy pearls slapped in gnarled knots near her hemline. If someone were going to kill her, she had at least tried to look her best while meeting her demise. But what would the Lord of Gorlachen think of faux pearls? His life was full of expensive jewels, the real thing. If faux pearls and inexpensive silver lame shoes were the best she could do, why should she care what he thought? She was tired of worrying about it. But why was she giving in to the idea that someone wanted to kill her? She was so very tired of thinking about it that she knew she was making herself sick. She didn't want to just let herself die casually, but what could she do about it?

Compliments were showered on her when she entered the dining room.

"What a marvelous hairdo," Mae Eldred said with longing. "It looks ravishing."

"You look lovely," Annalisa doted, gazing over the satin dress with a practiced eye.

They may be happy and enjoying themselves, but Julia treated everyone who spoke to her as though they were cold-blooded killers. She couldn't believe anything they said. Freckles and fuzzy blond hair might be considered cute, but they had never been considered "lovely." And her kinky hair--ravishing? Why was she receiving all of this attention? She was the rather dull daughter of a pair of high-luster Broadway actors.

John Eldred left Mae's side and rushed to hand Julia a glass of Glenlivet and soda. He made a small flourishing bow as he openly studied the beauty of her slim figure. His mild flirtations were usually carried on with a great lack of subtlety--the crossing of come-hither eye beams and a this-poor-man-needs-help-from-a-beautiful-woman-like-you approach.

The detective, Paul Hampton, scampered around to place a chair for her near the fireplace. His red-brown eyes flamed from the fire's reflection. "The room is not very warm," he said self-consciously, his eyes lingering on her plunging neckline. "You might be more comfortable near the fire."

"I'm quite comfortable, thank you," said Julia coldly. She hoped he didn't taken her comments at the abbey today too literally. On the other hand, when had a mild flirtation ever hurt anyone?

From across the room Nigel's eyes held hers as though they wanted to convey a message she was not quite getting. A warning about something? Himself? When he came toward her she gazed down at the knotted pearls and fingered them nervously, like she was seeing them for the first time. She felt his eyes follow her hands. Abruptly their eyes met.

"You remind me of our grandmother," he said. Then, realizing the implications, he laughed uncomfortably. "I mean in the way you use your hands. She always fingered the necklaces she wore when she was nervous." He seemed flustered, unable to think of anything interesting to say. His gaze was unnerving.

What Julia heard herself saying next was something she had not thought through at all.

"I have a surprise for you after dinner, cousin. Of course, I can't announce it because the other guests don't know your real identity, but I want you to know it's for you."

"Ah, the week has been full of surprises," he said, having regained his composure. "Now let's see. What would a lovely American girl plan as a surprise for a stodgy skinflint of an Englishman like myself?"

Heat rose in Julia's face. She was not surprised Hampton told him about their conversation. It was the kind of thing the two men chuckled over in private no doubt, making sport of women and their impossible ways in the process.

"Oh, *you're* not the stodgy Englishman," she said quickly. "Now you take Inspector Walpole. There is your stodgy Englishman."

"Yes, but effective," Nigel said, studying her face. "He's a man who won't be fooled for long."

"Meaning?" Julia stiffened.

"Meaning he'll solve this murder quickly. No one present here in the castle, including the servants, will escape his scrutiny. He's known for his ability to crack the toughest cases."

"So why are you telling me this? Has he talked you into believing *I* murdered Professor Quayle?"

"No, no. Nothing like that." His face colored again with anger. "He bloody well hasn't told me much of anything, Julia. Can't we have a simple conversation without all this ragging?"

"What do we have to say to each other?" she snapped. She left him wallowing in his anger and walked over to Jeremy and Sara. She wanted to make things right with them after the incident at the abbey. In such a close group bitter feelings were heightened and it seemed unnecessary. After all, whatever Rachel and Jeremy might have been involved in at the abbey wasn't her fault.

Sara wore an azure coat dress with dazzling rhinestone buttons. A mass of dark ringlets sprang from small combs at the top of her head. Her dark eyes gazed defiantly into Julia's then dropped to the glass of white wine she held.

"It was a beautiful abbey, wasn't it?" Jeremy said, his eyes resting on Julia's in a way that said,

"We understand each other, don't we?"

"Yes, quite lovely," Julia responded, meeting his gaze in acquiescence. "It was an afternoon to remember."

"Can I get you a chair?" he asked.

"No thanks, I think I'll make the rounds first."

Rachel entered the room looking ravishing in a hot pink crepe dress with an eggshell lace scarf caught by a pearl pin on one shoulder. Her slim legs were sheathed in lace hosiery. Julia thought she was easily the best looking woman in the room. She eyed Jeremy to see if he reacted in any way to Rachel's appearance. He glanced up when she walked by, said "hello," in a disinterested sort of way, then went back to doting on Sara. He must have come to realize he needed to watch his behavior from now on.

"Young Andrews may give Rachel the push by the time they get back to the States," Paul Hampton had come up behind Julia and spoke in her ear. "He may be married to Rachel, but he may have played his part with Sara Danes too well. He acts downright potty about the girl, doesn't he? She's a real looker."

Julia's breath caught. Poor Rachel. What was going to become of her if Jeremy threw her over? She changed the subject. "Look, Paul, would you do something for me? There's a cello at the end of one of those long halls leading away from the bedroom suites. Would you get it for me, but keep it out of Nigel's sight until I ask for it after dinner? Make sure the bow is with it." She came here to play the cello for Nigel, at his request, and she intended for him to hear it.

Only now did she consider the risks of playing an unfamiliar instrument, but on first sight of the cello she had an inexplicable feeling that it was played regularly. She had a good ear. If it needed a good tuning, she could tune it.

Paul seemed reluctant to leave the room. Julia suspected Nigel gave him instructions to keep a close eye on her. Finally she relaxed when she saw him disappear through the shadowy hall and hoped things would go as planned. Could she count on him? They were ready to sit down to dinner before he reappeared.

"I had to talk the servants out of checking with Lord Maltby about the cello," he whispered and shrugged. "I had to tell them it was the Lord's cousin who requested it. You jolly well don't run around picking things up at random in this bloody place."

"No, of course not," Julia said apologetically. "The thought didn't occur to me."

Now that the decision was made to play for Nigel, Julia began to pay attention to the food. For the first time since she arrived at the castle her appetite fit comfortably with the dazzling array of delicious foods served. A succulent crown rib roast with Yorkshire pudding made up the centerpiece. Colorful vegetable dishes were passed by formally dressed servants. Julia took a small serving of each one and ate ravenously.

Seated at the foot of the sumptuous table in this breathtakingly beautiful room, Julia found herself set back many centuries in history pretending to be the queen of a great and powerful castle. She could even feel the weight of a tiara chock full of heirloom rubies, emeralds, and diamonds perched regally on her important head. When she realized what she was doing she brought herself up short and glanced at Nigel. His Maltby gray eyes, dancing with firelight, were on hers. Her eyes darted away. Had he read her thoughts? Was he afraid she wanted to encroach on his wealthy lifestyle? If so, why did he invite her here? A creeping fear worked its way up her spine and left her hands as dead and cold as quick-frozen hams. How could she ever play a decent solo now?

Mountainous white-topped desserts arrived amid passionate cries of delight. Julia noticed Nigel turned his away. No wonder he was so slim. She followed suit and tried to think how to introduce her solo. But why introduce it? She would simply sit down, take plenty of time to tune the instrument, then play whatever came to mind.

She caught Paul Hampton's eye and motioned for him to bring in the cello. She took it from him and made her way up the steps to the minstrel gallery. Wasn't that where music was played in the Middle Ages? She placed her chair where she could see down on the dinner group and then searched in her purse for the chunk of resin she carried. She peered over the railing to watch the look on Nigel's face while she got herself ready to play.

If she expected the Lord of Gorlachen to make a show of emotion, such as delight that she was going to play, or fury over her having taken the liberty of moving the cello without his permission, she was disappointed. His face was a model of courtesy and breeding. He watched and waited with the rest of the guests while she prepared the instrument.

Looking for the first time down the satiny patina of the elegant honey-stained wood, Julia could see it was, indeed, a very fine instrument. She hoped to do it justice. She pulled the bow across the resin, taking her time to be sure everything was perfectly prepared. She posed her elbow and wrist and pulled the bow across the open strings. Then she relaxed the bow at her side while she waited for the deep rumbling tones to die away. It came as no surprise that the instrument needed little tuning.

She had not, until that very moment, decided what she would play. The smooth beauty of the wood was grained with what looked like long rivulets of water running from the top to pool smoothly near the bottom. She was instantly taken with the notion that her bow was a swan gliding across clear waters. Without giving it another thought she began to play.

The swelling deep-throated tones of the simple melody pulsed through the beautiful room with an aching rapture that transported Julia away from the group at the table to become the arching swan on a placid lake. She closed her eyes and swayed rhythmically with the sound as the bow bit dramatically into the strings, the music pulsating through her body like a beacon in a slow-moving current. She had never before played Saint-Saens' piece, *The Swan*, with such intensity. She stole a glance at Nigel. His eyes were riveted on hers, his head swaying slightly with the energy of the music. She quickly closed her eyes again.

The final high note seemed to hang in the air like an angelic wraith. She listened joyously until the last delicate sound fell away. When she finally opened her eyes, jerking herself back to reality, she found eight mesmerized listeners staring back at her from perfectly still relaxed bodies. Then, realizing the performance was finished, they all smiled at once and broke into a grateful round of applause.

Nigel jumped from his chair and sprang up the steps, his gray eyes misted with emotion. He moved close to her and spoke quietly.

"Julia, that was the most beautiful cello I've ever heard. You are, indeed, accomplished far beyond your years just as your father said. How I wish grandfather could have been here to hear it. Congratulations, my dear. This was grandfather's instrument, you know. It's a seventeenth-century Stradivarius. No one has ever played it quite like he did...except at this moment...except for you. Please accept it as a gift from him and myself."

Tears stung Julia's eyes. She looked down at the magic cello. Somewhere in the distant past she remembered being told her grandfather played. Yes..she remembered now. It was the day her father's face flushed with displeasure when she announced she wanted to learn the clarinet. He insisted she learn a stringed instrument, "*...and why not the cello, my dear? Your grandfather played.*" Julia followed his advice and seemed to take to the instrument quite naturally.

She could not accept the instrument, of course. Like the jewelry and a multitude of other things, it belonged here at Gorlachen, where, in these splendid rooms its music surpassed any she had ever heard. She looked for Nigel to explain it to him, but he had disappeared.

Julia was not sure what to do. She didn't want to appear ungrateful. She hurriedly accepted warm congratulations from the guests and promised she'd play again before they left. Then she scooped up the cello and bow and rushed from the dining room to return them to their resting place in the back hall.

Her backless stiletto shoes echoed with clickety-clacks as she clomped ungracefully up the front hall staircase, lifting the cello high so it could not possibly bang against the stones.

When she reached the upper hall the overhead candles were not lit. The glass-covered arrowslits at the ends of the passages let in only enough evening light to allow her to make her way. Nothing would deter her from immediately putting the magic cello back in its cradle.

For some unexplained reason the music moved her from a realm of fear and anxiety to one of inner calm and determination. She was neither frightened at being alone nor in a hurry.

She ambled along the dusky passages, a rising kinship with the past echoing around her. Her grandfather was a cellist who played at Gorlachen, *she* was a cellist who played at Gorlachen. *He* was a Maltby, *she* was a Maltby. For the first time she had some concept of what that meant, of the enduring bloodline reincarnating itself in each new generation. Suddenly all other thoughts melted away and it became terribly important to her to sustain her part in the ongoing Maltby family. Nigel could keep the cello, but she must keep Dunrose Manor. It belonged to her. She would keep it no matter what it meant to Nigel.

She was about to reach the end of the long hallway. Coming up on her right was a dark narrow passage that led to the servant's stairs and into the lower kitchen. She was struck with wonder at why the priceless instrument was kept in such an odd out-of-the-way place. She must ask Nigel about it.

She stepped over the rope and placed the cello in its cradle. When she started to turn...a *swish swish* of steps...a rush of breath as someone prepared to give her head a mighty blow. All went black.

Chapter 18

The next thing Julia knew she struggled awake amid a stir and bustle of startled voices and eager helping hands. She was at a loss to know where she was or what was going on. The air seemed miserably cold. Someone placed something soft under her head. Rachel's face was a dim blur over hers.

"Julia? Oh, my God, Julia, can you hear me?"

Rachel's pleading voice was like a shout through centuries of static. It came and went with the pounding in Julia's ears. She could hear her dinner companions whispering among themselves with fright as they tried to understand what happened. Pale excited faces swirled in indefinite patterns before her aching eyes. They all came running when they heard Rachel's screams.

"Who is it?" someone asked timidly as though they didn't want to know.

"What's happened? Do we have another murder here?" It was Mae Eldred's horrified voice.

Through the hubbub Julia heard quick footsteps approach. Paul Hampton's voice cut sharply through the haze.

"What's this about?" He took Rachel by the shoulders and moved her aside, then leaned over Julia and took hold of her wrist, touched her forehead. "What's happened here?" He stared vacantly at the blood in Julia's hair, blood splotched on her dress, blood in a pool on the floor.

"She...she was...she must have been returning the cello when someone attacked her," Rachel babbled, still in shock. "She wasn't in her room. I tried the door several times, then came looking for her and found her here on the floor in a pool of blood. Oh, Julia, please wake up." She began to sob hysterically.

Against her will, Julia closed her eyes, but she could hear Rachel's excited gasps and hoped she would not go to pieces before Julia could force her eyes open again.

"Is she dead?" Rachel whispered.

"No, but she's got a nasty cut there. How did this happen?" Anger filled Hampton's voice as he stared belligerently into Rachel's eyes. "When is this nonsense going to stop?"

"Why are you looking at me?" Rachel cried in anguish. "Surely you don't think...you couldn't possibly think...oh please, why would I do such a thing to this darling girl?"

Julia heard no response. With her eyes closed she could imagine how the group stood in a helpless huddle, gaping at Hampton and Rachel in horror through the failing light like charcoal caricatures of their former selves. The horror of it was that someone, perhaps someone right here within arm's length, tried again to kill her. What was going to be done about it?

"Shouldn't we get a doctor? Where is Inspector Walpole?" Annalisa whispered.

Julia tried to sit up. "I don't need a doctor. Just let me get to bed." With a heavy sigh she gave up trying to sit and let Paul Hampton lower her to the floor again.

"It's a bloody nuisance that the police can't seem to solve the simplest of crimes these days," John Eldred said from the background. "Where *is* Walpole? Why are all these women pottering about the castle in the dark without a man to protect them? It's a disgrace. I have a notion I could solve it all within twenty-four hours, given the chance."

"Why don't you do it then?" Mae's caustic voice cut through clearly. As usual, her comment was not about to stop John's mouth.

"Any woman who makes herself up like a clown and wears those bloody spiked heels deserves to finally trip and break her neck. It's perfectly clear that's what happened. Anyone could see it."

Mae looked at her husband as though he were some strange animal that had just escaped its cage.

"What do you know about it? Did you see something the rest of us didn't see?"

"Well...no, but it's not hard to figure out, eh?"

In spite of her wounds, Julia smiled. The pair waged a never-ending battle.

Chapter 19

The next time Julia was able to pry her eyes open she was heartened to see buttery yellow sunshine flooding the room while a lively sea breeze fluttered through lacy curtains at the window.

Nigel sat by the bed squeezing her hand until she wanted to scream for mercy. When her eyelids moved he leaned over her expectantly.

"My dear Julia," he whispered, "what's happening to us?"

Her eyes were too heavy to keep open. She listened to his soothing voice. An assembly of brilliant lights played through the spinning Milky Way of her sedated brain, while a bright red lacquered cello danced on snaky legs. A bodiless, dark, pinstriped suit grabbed it, and they danced merrily to an unknown tune. Suddenly the dancers disappeared and she heard a footstep, then a blow, but she didn't feel it. From a gigantic chandelier that whipped in circles at the end of a long chain, she watched herself sag and fall. Before she hit the floor she jerked violently and opened her eyes.

"Julia? Can you talk to me, Julia?"

She lay perfectly still while she listened to the *swish swish* of servant's uniforms as they passed back and forth in the hall. If Nigel wanted to kill her, why not simply finish her off and be done with it while he had her down? She was the only Maltby left to take his precious property.

She drifted away again, her brain whirling at a dizzying speed, bobbing around Nigel's worried face. Frustrated, she grabbed his hand.

"Did I play?" she asked, thoroughly confused. "I wanted it to be beautiful for you, but the instrument was taken away." She smiled wanly, frustrated at her tossed-salad thoughts. It seemed she played the solo a thousand years ago, and maybe she did. Drawing on her newly-assimilated bloodlines, she found the idea exhilarating. But Old Lady Gorlachen would take no notice. Time was her ally. Apparently she had tucked many a cello solo under her portly belt.

"It was the loveliest music I've ever heard," Nigel murmured against her tousled blood-dried hair. "Shhh. Just rest, my dear. The doctor gave you a very heavy sedative."

"I must get up," she said thickly. "There are only two days left. I want to see all of Dunrose Manor. I want to wander through her rooms and let her history seep into my bones."

"You shall. You shall, my Julia. I promise," he whispered.

When Julia awoke again it was to her name being called. Nigel was gone. A servant in a dark green uniform stood at her side with hot tea and two slices of the same thick dark whole-grain bread she had eaten at Dunrose Manor.

"Lord Maltby says to see to it that you fill your stomach, mum," the black-eyed young woman said matter-of-factly. She helped Julia sit up against a drift of plump lacy pillows and placed an ebony tray in front of her. A graceful silver vase held a perfect single mauve rose. It must have come from Dunrose Manor.

"Eat up now, or I'll be in big trouble," the girl said with a smile. "All we've 'eard in that bloody kitchen for weeks is 'take good care of Miss Maltby when she arrives,' but I'm afraid you've had a bit of a scare."

"What do you know about the goings-on?"

"I don't know nothing about it," the girl said, her questioning eyes snapping with wonder. "I didn't know about it 'til I 'eard all the screams in that ugly passageway. They're dark, ain't they, mum, them back passages? When a guest rings, I go up that main staircase, I do. I go back the same way, day or night."

"Do all the servants avoid the back hall?"

"Yes, mum, I'd say so. Especially at night. Them steps is treacherous, too steep for carrying heavy trays, and the halls are dark and scary."

"Scary how?"

"It's the cold and the silence, mum, and there was that man murdered in the darkness a few nights ago, and you was attacked as well. Everyone's scared." She thought for a moment. "Well, with the exception of Lord Maltby. He uses the back 'all and back steps all the time. He grew up playin' around this dingy old place, so nothin' scares 'im."

Julia considered it. Nigel would enjoy the ancient steep steps. He could never be persuaded to light the place. It was part of his continuum of history.

"Did you see anyone downstairs the night Mr. Quayle was murdered?"

"Oh, bloody goodness." She rolled expressive eyes dramatically. "Everyone was below stairs against the rules for one reason or another that night. We finally 'ad to call Lord Maltby back to the castle to look after things."

"Like what things?"

"Well, someone broke into Lord Maltby's safe in the office. He came over--and bloody goodness 'e was in a stew--but 'e said 'e didn't know what to do about it and to let Mr. 'ampton handle it since that's what 'e was hired for. Mr. 'ampton questioned all of us, then locked the office up until morning. My, we've never 'ad so much trouble with bed and breakfast guests. And that poor Inspector Walpole. He was beside 'imself with the nonsense of it."

"I see," Julia said, relaxing against the pillows. "Thank you for the tray."

"You're welcome, mum." The girl straightened the covers then hurried away, leaving Julia alone.

The events of the previous evening tumbled endlessly through her head. If she could only latch onto something, anything, that would give her a clue as to who waited soundlessly for her in the darkness of the servant's hall. A rigor shook her, sending a chill through her body that left her teeth rattling. It simply must have been Nigel. He was gone from the dining room and could not be located when she looked for him to explain her feelings about the cello. And according to the servant he came back to the castle from Dunrose Manor that first night while Julia was on her late-hour tour. Did he follow her to place blame for a murder? Was the robbery of the safe nothing more than a hoax? No one knew the castle as well as he did. *This castle is as familiar to me as the back of my hand.*

The words echoed through her brain. Julia looked doubtfully at the dark toast on her plate. She could not bring herself to eat it. Perhaps she needed a food taster for edibles that came from Dunrose Manor. A light tap on the door interrupted her journey into the sorry depths of medieval poisonings.

"Come in."

Paul Hampton, bearing a cut glass vase bursting with tiny blue-and-white flowers Julia could not put a name to, stuck his head in the door.

"How we doing?" His red-brown eyes were black in the blue-tinted light shining through the stained glass lampshade. Julia tucked the antique quilt higher around her thin white nightie as his eyes lingered on her bodice. She had paid scant attention to the fact that he was actually quite handsome. Leaving the hall door open, he strolled over to the bed, set the flowers on the bedside table, and looked her over. "Feeling better?"

"I'm getting my head back," she smiled. "It's full of bubbles and other strange shapes, but I think I'm coming around."

"You had a nasty fall there," he said with concern. "When are you going to start telling me when you're up to something, Miss Maltby? Why didn't you ask *me* to return the cello instead of wandering those bloody cold passages alone in the dark? I'll probably get sacked for not being able to keep up with you."

Julia laughed at his self-deprecation. It didn't suit him. "I'll put in a good word for you with Nigel."

"In all seriousness, Miss Maltby, do you have any notion who attacked you, or why someone might want to do such a thing?"

"Wouldn't I say if I did?"

"Did you hear any noises, recognize a voice, an odor such as perfume or shaving lotion, clothing, shoes, anything? Please think it over carefully."

"I was aware of absolutely nothing. I placed the cello in its cradle and started to turn when I heard a swish behind me, then everything went black."

"Did you pass someone in the hall? A servant perhaps? Anyone at all?"

"No one. But the hall to the kitchen steps joins the longer hall near the cello. Someone must have waited there in the darkness."

He sat in the red plush chair, pressed the tips of his fingers together, and they regarded each other solemnly. Finally Julia worked up enough courage to ask the unaskable.

"Mr. Hampton, do you think my cousin might have invited me here to kill me?" She swallowed hard at the thought. "He talks about protecting me, but there are reasons why he might like to dispose of me."

She watched Hampton's head jerk slightly in surprise as his eyebrows raised in a questioning look.

"What reasons?"

If he had not thought of this aspect of the case she was glad to bring it up for consideration. She thought it out carefully before she answered. "You see, I inherited Dunrose Manor from my father. Nigel lives there and is quite fond of the place. If I were out of the way he could live in it as long as he likes without having to worry about me taking it over. Also, I'm supposed to inherit several pieces of family heirloom jewelry. I have seen nothing of it yet. Then at the abbey this afternoon I think someone tried to kill me by dropping a rock from the wall."

"Oh, please, you're being dramatic, Miss Maltby," he said testily. "Those rocks are not what you'd call stable. Didn't you see the signs warning against them? There were people clamoring about all over the bloody place. Any slight vibration might have shaken one of them down."

"I'm not being dramatic. It's the truth," Julia whimpered when she saw how he discounted her experience.

"Then why didn't you tell me earlier? It's becoming harder and harder for me to take your complaints seriously, I must say." He paused. "I suppose you didn't tell Walpole either." He watched her shake her head. "Well...now we have no way of finding incriminating evidence, do we? There may have been dozens of people through that abbey since our group left."

Julia hated the way he was able to make her feel guilt when she was not guilty, to embarrass her and make her feel ashamed.

"I didn't want to create a scene." Neither did she want to elaborate enough to tell Hampton she could trust no one. She was a prime suspect in Quayle's murder and yet Quayle must have been the one who placed the film in her care. Until Walpole returned with the pictures and she saw the importance of them for herself she would speak of it to no one.

Hampton studied her wearily, then threw his arms up in a giving-up gesture. "I suppose what you're saying is a possibility, but come on, luv, Lord Maltby is my employer. It would be bloody ironic, would it not, if he had engaged me to suspect *him*?" He pressed his fingertips up and down in spider push-ups again. He was deep in thought. "Quite honestly, Julia, I find it far more likely that you're trying to protect someone."

She stared at him, feeling immense fright. "Who could I possibly be protecting?"

His eyes rested on hers, sizing her up for the truth.

"You haven't told me everything," he said like a jealous husband. "I feel there's something you're holding back. Nigel told you about our suspicions concerning your friend, Rachel Givens. What do you know about that?"

"Absolutely nothing." The subject, as always, brought a bitter taste to her mouth. "I have never seen nor heard anything from Rachel that would in any way indicate involvement in jewelry heists, or that she came to Gorlachen for any other reason than to enjoy a holiday."

"Were you aware when you brought Rachel to Gorlachen with you that she's married to Jeremy Andrews?"

"No."

"Have you asked her about it, like why she kept it from you?"

Julia hesitated. Now that she thought about it she wondered why she hadn't asked. "No, I haven't talked to her about it. Nigel implied you were hired to implement some sort of plan to catch Rachel and Jeremy at whatever it is you suspect them of. He asked me not to show his hand, so I didn't."

"Smart girl. Your full cooperation surely will be needed to carry out those plans. I must point out, Miss Maltby, that both Rachel and Jeremy were the first to reach the spot in the hall where you were attacked last night. The person or persons who discover the victim are often the perpetrators of the crime. People really aren't very original, you know. I can attest to it from many cases I've worked on." He paused while he considered it, his dark eyes wandering back to her bodice. "How did Rachel know you were in the back hall? Did you tell her you were about to return the cello?"

"No, I didn't tell anyone. Don't forget Mae Eldred was leaning over me too. I happen to know first hand she was downstairs the night Quayle was murdered. Why isn't she a suspect, or her husband, John? And there were Sara Danes and Annalisa Bowers, and...and all of those servants, and...." her voice faded away as she realized from the look on his face that she was getting nowhere.

"There, luv, as you can see, the Inspector and I have a difficult task ahead of us. We're considering every possibility."

Hampton got up and walked to the door. He smiled as though to signal an end to the grilling. "I'll leave you now to rest. I'll pop in again tomorrow. Think it over carefully, and if anything comes to you about last night please let me know at once. I'll fill Walpole in on our conversation when he gets back from the mainland. Pleasant dreams, my dear. Do keep the door locked through the evening."

When he was gone Julia got up and snapped the lock in place. There would be no pleasant dreams however. She had no intention of going back to bed. She intended to dress and go downstairs to dinner. The mere thought of being left alone all evening petrified her. Whoever wanted that film was not going to give up easily. She could only hope Inspector Walpole would show up with the finished slides, and soon.

Julia hated to admit, even to herself, that she was afraid to walk to dinner with Rachel, so she ignored the familiar tap on the door and walked down the long dark staircase alone ten minutes later.

Chapter 20

In the dining room the women made a fuss over Julia's injuries. She assured them she was getting on just fine and would be like new tomorrow.For her own comfort, she chose an informal soft blue cashmere dress and simple black pumps with French heels to wear for the evening.

The men stopped their conversations to look her over. She was not sure whether they admired her looks or if they were merely curious about the girl who played the cello solo and got a clout on the bean for her efforts.

"What are you doing out of bed?" Nigel said in a whisper at her side. "I specifically ordered Hampton to make sure you were locked in safely for the night for complete rest."

"He did exactly as you told him. You're awfully hard on the poor man, Nigel. I run my own life, you know."

"Hard on him? I thought you didn't even like him."

"To the contrary, I think he's really quite charming," she said, remaining aloof.

He looked at her helplessly, but was forced to conclude the conversation when the Eldreds and Paul Hampton, with drinks in hand, strolled over to them. John Eldred had clearly worked himself into an unhappy state of fuzzy reality and was letting the fake Maltby know about it.

"Oh I say, Maltby, what's being accomplished in this investigation?

Your man, Walpole, was downright hostile to this lovely lady in an interview in our room yesterday." He squeezed Mae until she grimaced. "Now I ask you, does this sweet thing look like a woman who could murder a man?"

"Please, John, don't bore these people with your nonsense," Mae sniped.

"Just look at that lower lip tremble. She doesn't look a day over thirty when she's angry, eh?" he teased.

No one could miss the look of utter contempt that flickered swiftly across Mae's face as she glared at him, then quickly looked away. If looks could kill, John would be a dead man.

"Sorry John," Nigel's stand-in said, trying to live up to his role of Nigel Maltby with ease, "Walpole has a job to do, and we'll have to allow him to do it his way. He'll let us know when things are in hand."

Julia decided Paul Hampton was getting better at being Lord Maltby. He carefully copied Nigel's speech habits and the modulated tones of the well educated, but he was not exactly a gentleman in his ways. She could not quite put her finger on specifics. It was an attitude. In spite of it, she thought he was doing a commendable job for whatever it was worth. She chose a chair against the wall to enjoy her glass of pre-dinner wine. She didn't want anyone coming in behind her.

The array of colorful china and glittering gold and silver utensils that caught everyone else's eye with pleasure, seemed cold and forbidding to her. She watched the other guests having a wonderful time. They didn't seem to be particularly worried about the murder. Why was she singled out to protect a nebulous roll of film? Her vacation was nearly over and she was not enjoying a single moment of it.

Rachel, Jeremy, and Sara were having a good laugh over something Julia could not hear. Paul Hampton and Nigel stood near the door grinning at each other over some sort of private joke, probably about how stupid and inept they thought her to be. Only Mae and John Eldred stood apart frowning at each other.

Annalisa arrived at the last minute wearing a clinging black satin dress and matching pumps with a sprinkle of dazzling diamonds across the toes. Whether the diamonds were real or not Julia couldn't tell. The shiny black of the dress made glittering coals of her dark eyes. In spite of a bent toward coarseness, there was an attractiveness about her that was difficult to describe. For some unaccountable reason, Julia felt a dislike for her. She watched her walk straight to Nigel, her thick hips moving tantalizingly in a sexy, quivering undulation. She smiled broadly and gave Nigel a strong hug with a quick kiss on the cheek. He seemed eager to return the caress. Then he abruptly turned from her and crossed the room to Julia.

"Since you felt like coming downstairs, I've planned a surprise for *you*," he said softly. "You'll understand pretty soon."

All sorts of ideas leaped from Julia's busy imagination. Was he going to admit to his charade, announce who hit her on the head and murdered Professor Quayle? Or perhaps it was something more personal. Maybe he was going to announce his engagement to Annalisa. Obviously they were quite fond of each other. Julia wondered if Annalisa lived here in the castle, or maybe at Dunrose Manor. Her heart quickened at the thought and brought a warm flush to her cheeks. Why should that upset her? What Nigel did or did not do with his life was his own business. His American cousin was merely a temporary and troublesome interruption. Whatever he planned, the evening, she hoped, would move her one day closer to getting away from Castle Gorlachen. She looked around for Walpole. Where was he with the photographs?

A grand dinner of roast duck with orange sauce and heaps of delicately flavored fruits and vegetables was served. Waves of satiny candlelight jabbed long pointed fingers, like a modern gyrating dance team, into dark corners, charging the atmosphere with an ethereal quality.

A hubbub of conversation around her made it difficult for Julia to concentrate on any one group. Jeremy complained again about the cameras, Rachel was concerned about the stormy weather that seemed to make the tide highly unpredictable for the return to the mainland and the train trip to Heathrow. "That's if we're allowed to leave here on time," she concluded.

Julia listened patiently while John Eldred rattled off ragtag bits of romantic poetry in his wife's honor, often attributing them to the incorrect poet. Apparently Nigel was tired of correcting him. The more embarrassed Mae became as he continued to shoot off his mouth, the more John seemed to enjoy himself.

"Maybe he'll ask her to remove her clothes and dance on the table for us," Jeremy Andrews piped up. The words had an unkind ring to them.

John Eldred was too drunk to comprehend the dig, but Mae understood it all too well. She turned on Jeremy with fury.

"It's hell to get old," Mr. Andrews. "You'll have to face the fact that part of life is, regrettably, old women like myself. Perhaps your smart tongue will swallow you up someday."

"Well, I didn't mean...." Jeremy's face flushed a deep red.

"I know what you meant. Keep your insults to yourself."

Jeremy sat back in his chair and glowered at the floor.

"Where are you going when your stay at Gorlachen ends, Mae?" Julia asked, hoping to defuse the unpleasantries. She hoped Mae would describe something spectacularly interesting. The poor woman deserved it.

"To Aberdeen. My...."

John's hand shot out to pat Mae's knee. "Are you going to tell it my dear, or should I? You know the trouble you have with details, my darling." He turned importantly to Julia. "Indeed, we've traveled the world--Paris, Rome, Venice, the Danube. One must these days to get a reasonable overview of things, eh? So what better idea than to travel one's own country? We hope to be in Aberdeen sometime soon for Mae's niece's wedding, but if Walpole doesn't get this murder solved, we won't get there on time. Boring fellow, what? It's a crime how bloody inefficient the police are these days."

Julia hardly heard him. She was spellbound watching Nigel's gestures and pleased facial expressions while he explained historical details about his favorite subject, Castle Gorlachen, to Jeremy Andrews. It was his attempt to pull his guests away from arguments--probably more arguments than he ever imagined would take place at Gorlachen. His body moved with a lithe grace. He was handsomely dressed in dark trousers, white shirt, and a brocade vest of soft grays and pale mauve. Occasionally his eyes sought hers.

121

When their eyes met, Julia quickly glanced down to watch dancing bubbles rise and burst in her glass of wine. When she looked up again she saw Nigel give Paul Hampton a nod. Hampton left the room and was gone for some time.

Presently he came back and sat down again at the head of the table. He nodded to Nigel. Then Nigel jumped up and disappeared. It was like a game of musical chairs. When he returned, he carried the magic cello and its bow.

Julia cringed with fear. The events of last night raced menacingly before her eyes. She did not feel up to playing this evening. She hated to play at a time when she felt she could not play well. How unbelievably thoughtless of Nigel to expect it. She rose to excuse herself. She fully intended to behave rudely and disappear up the stairs.

Instead, she melted slowly back into her chair. To her surprise, Nigel seated himself comfortably in front of the group with the cello in position. He pulled the bow across the strings. With great deliberation he tuned the instrument and let the last deep discordant tones rumble away before he leaped commandingly into the first movement of Saint-Saens' Concerto in A Minor. The tones were crisp and vital. Even without an orchestral background, the music filled the room. He played with such voracious energy Julia found herself teetering on the edge of her chair, expectantly, as the familiar music swelled and ebbed, swelled and ebbed, leaving her breathless, as though a tight blanket of music had wrapped itself like a constrictor around her body, squeezing her very breath away. He played so much better than she that she was embarrassed at her own efforts.

She closed her eyes and let the music encompass her. Now she knew beyond a doubt that the magic cello must never be removed from the castle. The ancient stone walls were steeped in its magnificent tones.

Nigel ended the movement as vigorously as he began it.

When the last sound died away, Julia quickly opened her eyes. They settled with speculation on Nigel. So he was the one who played the instrument regularly. She was deeply puzzled. He obviously had a fondness for it, and yet he saw fit to give it to her. Perhaps he made the expansive gesture because he was going to do away with her so she would not be around to remove it from the castle.

While Julia puzzled, Annalisa was on her feet shouting, "Bravo. Bravo, darling. You've played exquisitely." The others joined her in a hearty round of applause.

"I jolly well hope we're not all expected to produce something like this," John Eldred said. "I'm afraid you'll find me sadly lacking. My wife's beauty will have to suffice for the both of us."

Julia glared at him for spoiling the mood. She wondered if he would survive the stay without someone finally punching his lights out. She found her own fist doubled over a few times.

She hung back to allow others to congratulate Nigel, then she walked closer and listened intently while Annalisa hugged him and made over him..."And to think, darling, you were going to give up playing because you thought you would never play as well as your grandfather. Such rubbish," she said, cooing like a mother hen.

Nigel beamed like a child over her lavish display of affection. He loosened himself from her grasp and began putting things away. Timidly Julia approached him.

"Thank you, Nigel," she said, feeling for the right words. "You play expertly. Thank you for a beautiful memory of Castle Gorlachen. I will cherish it always." She hesitated while he studied her face. "I've not had the chance to thank you for offering me the cello, but I could never remove it from the castle."

"Why not? It's an unmatched instrument. It's alive and has reasoning powers of its own. I know, because it makes my playing sound better than it really is. You'd better take it. You'll never find a cello with a purer tone."

"Thanks, but I'll pass. Gorlachen would mourn the loss." She smiled sadly. "And what makes me think you would miss it a great deal yourself? You might have told me you play. Maybe I would have hesitated to make such a fool of myself last night...." A massive lump in her throat choked off the words and kept her from finishing her thoughts. She ran from the room and stumbled up the staircase.

"Julia, wait," she heard from behind her, but she pressed on up the steps. Nigel could keep his cello and his Annalisa. She didn't care.

As she hurried up the hall she could see the door to her room hanging slack on its hinges before she got to it. She remembered carefully latching it before she left for dinner. She eased it open and peered inside. The lamp was lit. She pushed the door wider so she could see the full room. Then she got down on her knees in the hall to search under the bed. She left the armoire door open so no one could hide in it, but now it was closed. It had become a game, hadn't it? Who could outwit whom?

She had to smile. The room had been taken apart again. A telltale bottle of nail varnish was overturned on the dresser. Someone was, indeed, desperate for that film.

Instantly she froze in place, alerted by a slight sound, something soft scraping against the wall at the turning in the hall. She caught sight of a shadow, then heard stealthy footsteps moving away down the back passage. She ran to the turn. Before she could get there she heard a door latch. The hall was empty. Who left the dining room before her? She quickly tried to recreate the scene before she could forget the details....

She talked to Nigel after Annalisa moved away. Annalisa...Annalisa left the dining room before her. She was at the abbey, and she appeared with the others in the hall when Julia was lying on the floor bleeding. *Oh, God. Where was Walpole?* She jumped inside the room and snapped the lock into place.

Chapter 21

Nigel and Paul Hampton checked Julia's door to see that it was locked, then they strolled companionably down the back stairs to the path that crossed the garden to Dunrose Manor. Dusk glowed in the last rays of sun reflected from brilliant shrimp and mauve-tinged clouds. Roosting birds kicked up a fuss in a copper beech near the wall.

Nigel breathed deeply of the salty air spiked with an earthy sweetness from blooms in the garden. He had always loved to walk in the garden at dusk, its reds, purples, pinks, and creams flowing graciously from one enchanting bloom to another like a soft-edged watercolor.

However, tonight he was having difficulty trying to iron out the deeply-grooved frown that came from trying to figure out what had happened at dinner earlier in the evening. He thought Julia would be pleased that he played the cello for her, but instead, it seemed to have upset her. What did he do? He was so sorry he alienated her. She was correct when she said he played expertly. He certainly did hit all the correct notes, but he felt he hadn't played *well*, not with the compelling emotion and liquidity that flowed from her bow. As discouraging at it was, it was nothing he wanted to talk to Hampton about.

"What advances are being made on this case, Hampton? Are there any real suspects?"

"We're doing everything we can," Paul said. "Forensics found no prints on the statue that killed Quayle. We don't even know *why* he was killed. Walpole has been on the mainland for a full day now checking out the man's background to see if he was acquainted with any of the guests before they came here. I'm to delve more fully into the background of our American friends, Rachel Givens and Jeremy Andrews, which I'm in the process of doing. I need some further answers from the FBI. Something may break on that yet.

"Security reported that Rachel was with Miss Maltby on the grounds immediately after she left the manor house this morning. All that means is that they met outside the house. You and I both know your cousin was with you when the prowler was reported. Do you suppose she was keeping your attention while Rachel looked for valuables in the house? We need an answer to that question. Then, of course, Rachel and Jeremy were the two hovering over Julia when I got to her in the back hall last night. Do they want to get rid of her because she knows too much? And how did they know where she was? Julia said she didn't tell Rachel she was about to return the cello. I was keeping an eye on her, and even I missed it when she left the dining room."

Nigel immediately thought of how hard he was being on the "charming" Mr. Hampton. "It's not your fault, Hampton. She's a girl with a mind of her own. She's a Maltby for heaven's sake. She's not about to check in with anyone on her whereabouts."

"You can say that again, sir. She's like trying to keep track of a bar of slippery soap." Then Hampton grinned. "A fetching bar of slippery soap nevertheless."

Nigel gave him a sharp look. Was Hampton cultivating a romantic interest in Julia? What was all that rubbish Julia dealt him about how hard he is being on Hampton?

They walked down the gravel path in silence, Nigel kicking a rock ahead of him as he went, unexplained anger seething through him. "You really don't need to protect me, Hampton. I'm perfectly capable of taking care of myself. I'd rather you stayed in the castle and kept an eye on Julia. I don't know if someone tried to kill her at the abbey, or if she's just exaggerating, as you say, but the thought petrifies me. If she becomes frightened no telling what she might decide to do. We can't allow anything to happen to her, do you understand, Hampton?

Absolutely *nothing* is to happen to Julia. I could never forgive myself if it did."

"There's another thing, sir," Hampton said, ignoring Nigel's emotional outburst. "Julia was in the sculpture gallery the night Quayle was killed. We can't overlook it to be quite honest about it. She admitted it. And if someone wanted to kill her, why didn't they finish the job at the abbey? Who's to say she didn't set that up herself, perhaps with Andrews and Rachel? I'm afraid I'd have to say that, at the moment, Walpole and I have come to the conclusion that she's a prime suspect."

Nigel swung around and glared at him. "That's the silliest thing I ever heard, Hampton. She told us why she was in the sculpture gallery. That was our fault, yours and mine, for trying to pull off this silly charade. She got lost looking for the branding irons. Someone used the knowledge of her presence in the gallery to set her up. Even I can figure that out."

"Who, then, sir? Rachel Givens? She's the only person Julia knew well enough to confide in at that point besides yourself. Rachel might have worked her over in the passage, but was interrupted by someone, possibly one of the other guests who doesn't want to get involved, then screamed to make it look like she just found her."

"Has Walpole questioned Rachel about her past?" Nigel asked.

"Only in a roundabout way. We didn't want to tip our hand, you see. It's a funny thing, sir. When he asked her if she had ever been in any kind of trouble with the police, she went into a fury and told him right out, 'go straight to hell,' she said, and a few other choice things besides. She's a self-possessed woman, that one."

A mental image of the Inspector, retreating smugly into his silent cryptic world of clues and analysis in the face of Rachel Givens's fury, suddenly struck Nigel as highly entertaining. He laughed aloud.

"Something wrong, sir?"

"No. No, it's nothing. Now what about Jeremy Andrews?"

"I won't test your hearing with what he told us to do, sir. Tall handsome American men aren't easy people to deal with. They're natural bluffers who hate being called on the carpet. By the way, Miss Maltby told me she ran onto Andrews and Miss Danes making love in the shadows of the abbey this afternoon."

127

"What? Julia told you something that personal?" Nigel stopped abruptly in the path, shocked at the thought of it. Why didn't Julia tell him instead? "Would you say Andrews is playing his part a little too thoroughly? I mean, if he and Rachel are in this thing together as man and wife, why would he risk that kind of behavior? Good Lord, right out there on the abbey grounds where his wife or some other member of the party could stumble over them?"

"I know it's hard to understand, but maybe he wants his relationship with Miss Danes to appear cemented so the real facts remain hidden. He wouldn't be the first to think up such a scheme.

I can remember a case at one of the big houses where a young man--a regular servant in the kitchen--wanted the butler's job when the butler retired. The valet to the Master, several cuts in importance above the kitchen help, also wanted the job. He did every underhanded thing he could to draw unpleasant attention to the kitchen servant so he would be chosen over him. Unfortunately, the head maid figured out what was happening, threatened to tell the Master, and the valet murdered her."

Nigel had no patience with extraneous stories. "Let's get on with it, Hampton. What about the Eldreds?" Why was he going through all of this? None of it made sense.

"If you'll pardon me, sir, speaking of silliness, the Eldreds are a pair to draw to. Eldred is really quite a nice chap when he's with other men, but you let a woman come into the room, especially an attractive woman, and he loses all sight of himself. He runs off at the mouth until he looks a complete fool, poor sod. I don't think he likes his wife much or he wouldn't go through all that nonsense to embarrass her about her beauty, or lack of it, and maybe he didn't like Quayle either. He appeared to be irate over Quayle having touched Mae. There are men, even if they don't like their wives very well, who won't stand for another man moving in on them. And then you have to consider that both Mae and John were downstairs at the time of Quayle's murder. We have to take that into consideration."

They strolled in silence for a time, Nigel pondering the problems presented by his roster of guests. "Are we going to let these people leave day after tomorrow? There's a new wave of bed and breakfast guests arriving on the weekend. If too many stay on, they'll need to flow over into Dunrose Manor. I can't bear the thought of it."

"I'll talk to Walpole about it tomorrow. Goodnight, sir," Hampton said. He gave Nigel a commiserating pat on the shoulder, then turned and headed down the path to the castle.

"Hampton," Nigel called.

Hampton swung around to look at him. "Yes, sir?"

"Take good care of her, will you, please?"

"Yes, sir," Hampton responded. He turned again and walked on down the path.

Nigel plunked down heavily on the top step of the manor house porch. Why had his life suddenly gone sour? A murder in the castle, a disguise designed to catch a thief that left egg on his face, an attempt on Julia's life, and finally his alienating her by playing the cello for her. What was he doing wrong? From now on he must keep his cello playing to himself.

It occurred to him that he never had the kinds of problems he now had until Julia Maltby entered his life. Did she lie to him and she was involved in a sinister plot with Rachel and Jeremy Andrews to swindle him in some way? She brought the two along. But what about Quayle? What could their interest be in him? Granted, Quayle was a bore with all of his unsought lectures, but that didn't call for killing him. Nothing made sense anymore.

He got up and walked around the gravel path that led to the big house's back entry. It was more than fifteen years since anyone entered Dunrose Manor through the Tudor-paneled front doors, and a shame it was. Such a beautiful old home deserved to be loved and petted.

He turned abruptly and retraced his path to the verandah. He covered the wide stone steps in a few short hops like he did when he was a child and came here with his grandmother.

The oversized black iron key lay hidden under one of the high shutters. It fit smoothly into the heavy wrought iron lock. With grating squeaks and a few minor complaints the door opened.

He stepped inside the high entry hall. A sour odor of abandonment and neglect hit him in a way that suddenly terrified him. How did he allow this elegant old lady to fend for herself for such a long time? Why did he neglect her when he knew how much he enjoyed her with his grandmother as a youth? He must put it right as soon as he could afford it.

It was quite dark inside the entry. He groped overhead for the long light cord. An eerie golden glow from a bare web-coated bulb high in mahogany beams did little to cheer him. He wondered what became of the massive frosted fixture that used to hang there. A handsome staircase of dark-finished oak gave the narrow entry a spectacular focal point. One of the problems with the house, he decided, was that the ceilings were too bloody high and dark for comfort. Perhaps his first project must be a lighter coat of paint between beams.

He stepped into the great hall. The place was as cluttered as his grandmother's jewelry box. She came from the height of the Victorian era when collections and doodads were the home's main accouterments. Knickknacks, silver collections, creamy pots and pitchers, and decorative porcelain pieces were just a few of the items that seemed to rocket through the room. Large and cumbersome pieces of stuffed furniture splashed with colorful floral designs were arranged in conversational groupings on several large and somewhat threadbare oriental carpets.

Discouragement at the manor house's poor condition shook him. Just as quickly as his desire to refurbish it came, his interest in it faded. He lived alone. There was no need for extravagance. He turned off the light, wandered outside, turned and locked the door.

He used only a few of the many available rooms in the back of the house on the ground floor. They originally were servants' quarters. Upstairs he redid his grandparents's master suite in its original Chippendale style, copying from early photographs. It included the large bedroom, a dressing room with an oversized walk-in closet, and a bathroom as spacious as the living room in most homes. There were five more bedrooms upstairs, and a faded arrogant ballroom with the works; Victorian crystal chandeliers and moth-eaten, red velvet swag draperies that matched a jumble of shabby red overstuffed pieces gathered around gilt-finished tables.

130

Besides the rooms he used downstairs, there were three mammoth parlors, a music room with a collection of very fine cellos, a library filled with several hundred leather volumes, an assortment of various-sized kitchens, butler's pantries, laundry rooms, and a dining room that rivaled the one in the castle for beauty. He must remember to show it to Julia.

Abruptly he realized he was talking to himself. He must stop this absurd vacillating. It was downright disorienting. One minute he decided Julia was responsible for the problems at the castle, the next minute he was planning ways to entertain her, to watch those blue-gray Maltby eyes widen with pleasure. He could not figure her out, that was sure. Worst of all, he could not figure himself out.

He locked the house and went upstairs. After rigorous exercise and a comforting shower, he stretched out on the bed with arms beneath his head and stared blankly at the paneled roof.

He was never able to fully decided what he wanted to do with his life. Music was his first love, but it was difficult to perform when one lived in an isolated manor house on an island off the coast of Northumberland. Yet that was where he wanted to be. He was not used to living around crowds, and he had no desire to start now.

Money was no problem for him. What was there to own that he could not buy if he wanted it? But was that all there was ever going to be in his life? The routine of worrying over investments and public duties, hours of cello practice, and intense exercise for good health clearly were no longer enough to satisfy him.

There had been women in his life. At one point Annalisa held some fascination for him, but he knew throughout the two years of their close association that she was not the one he would marry. She was entirely too dependent on wealth and a large contingent of family members to make decisions for her. He didn't need a woman he had to pamper either monetarily or emotionally. Annalisa was realistic enough to understand his position, and when he relayed his thoughts to her they quit their romance and became pleasant friends instead.

Then there was the beautiful Victoria Howard, an actress with a promising career. Her rare dark beauty captured him from the moment

131

he laid eyes on her. He fall hard and was crushed when she confessed to being pregnant with another man's child. They broke it off, and she seemed so pitiful when she begged him to tell her what happened to their love, and why, if they loved each other so deeply, they could not raise the child as their own. It was an unhappy time for her, but he realized then and there that he no longer, and possibly never had had any desire for a permanent relationship.

He told her his feelings, and she sobbed hysterically until it was time to go. He watched dispassionately as she left Dunrose Manor and waved goodbye to him through the window of a long white chauffeured car as it moved slowly through the main gates. He ignored her subsequent telephone calls and never saw her again. Within a few short weeks he completely forgot her and was surprised when, at times, she suddenly surfaced in a dream or through some other scrap of memorabilia that his mind conjured unexpectedly.

In spite of how he tried to avoid it, his eyes were pulled time and again to the photograph of the petite blue-eyed girl with the long untamed blond hair. When he was a child playing alone he wished Julia could come to play. He had photographs of her then, too, and kept them on his dresser, studying them and trying to imagine what she was like. When he asked his grandmother, she told him that Julia was very much like himself, a Maltby through and through. Somehow his father understood his longing, and before his death, paved the way for him and Julia to meet again. How excited he was the day he met her in the hall and saw how comely she was.

He envisioned her leaning gracefully over the cello, as lovely and sensual as the alluring pink lady on his mother's conch-shell cameo. She played masterfully for him. What if she decided to stay on, live in Dunrose Manor, and insist that he move? Worse yet, what if she decided to sell it? How could he handle it?

Then the thought that he tried to crowd from his mind suddenly leaped out at him, refusing to be ignored any longer. What if Julia were here, right now, lying beside him? He jumped up, startled, his stiffened body suffering at the thought of her. He pulled on a blue sweat suit and ambled restlessly through the house for the next several hours, assessing its need for repairs while haunting strains of *The Swan* coursed fiercely through his body.

When he saw the first rays of dawn at the windows he gave up all thoughts of getting any sleep, dressed in gray trousers and a black and white sweater, and went to his office in the castle.

Chapter 22

Sleep eluded Julia. She was hungry. After tossing and turning for two hours or more she got up and pulled the bell rope. A short time later a servant knocked on the door.

"Who is it?" Julia asked.

"Maid service," a lilting voice said.

Julia opened the door a crack. After the attack she would never feel safe again. A tall homely woman with a long straight nose peered curiously from under a white starched cap.

"What can I do for you, mum?" she asked politely.

"Is it possible to get something to eat at this hour?"

"Usually not, mum," the woman said crisply, "but for you, anything. Lord Maltby said, 'give my cousin, Julia, whatever she wants when she wants it.' We're prepared, mum."

"I'd like a cup of tea and wheat toast, please."

Julia smiled. Power was a wonderful thing. Why hadn't it been *her* father who inherited the castle? She waited while the woman disappeared down the long empty passage, then she sat down at the mahogany dressing table to varnish her nails. She hoped she would be leaving Gorlachen soon. Romantic notions of manor houses, handsome cousins, and bejeweled tiaras were lost to her now. She obviously did not belong here.

She shuddered when she recalled how her meager musical efforts were dwarfed by Nigel's superior cello playing. Nor was she the one to hold some sort of precious past in her hands in the form of invaluable jewelry for future generations. She wanted so much to make a good impression at Gorlachen, but instead, someone disliked her so much they wanted to kill her. The whole thing was mind-boggling. She heard steps at the door.

"Your tray, mum."

The door opened and the maid whisked by her with the tray. To Julia's surprise, Rachel stepped inside the room behind her.

"What do *you* want, Rachel?" Julia asked coldly. She eyed a heavy copper pitcher on the table near the bed and wondered how easily she could get to it to defend herself if necessary.

"I need to talk to you, hon. I've been worried sick about you. May I stay a while?"

Julia heard the maid say good night and watched helplessly as she went out, leaving Julia alone with Rachel. She tried to shake off a chill that left her trembling inside. How ironic it was that perhaps the only real thing she had to fear at Castle Gorlachen she brought along with her.

"I...I'm very tired. I was going to have a snack and get some sleep."

"Go ahead, eat your toast. I ate twice as much as I needed at dinner. The food is marvelous. I do love all of those vegetables. I don't know what those people who claim the English are poor cooks are talking about." She stretched and yawned. "The first thing I'll have to do when I get home is shed about ten pounds."

In spite of herself, Julia could not help but smile. Rachel was always, and unnecessarily, worried about her weight.

"Now," Rachel said, "let's talk about you. Who hit you? Come on, you can tell a friend. I saw you leave the dining room when you finished playing your solo and came to congratulate you, but I couldn't find you anywhere. I couldn't believe my eyes when I saw you crumpled in the hall in a pool of blood." She threw her arms up in despair. "Are you sure John Eldred wasn't correct? Are you sure you didn't slip on those skinny little silver heels and hit your head? I mean, isn't that possible, sweetie? Maybe you just don't remember it. Honest to God, hon, when I got to you the place was deserted. After thinking it over, I don't see how anyone could possibly have hit you and escaped before I got there...I couldn't have been more than a couple of minutes behind you. Anyway, the next thing I remember is one long piercing scream after another--mine."

"If I knew the answers to your questions, obviously I'd have told the inspector and we'd have the problem solved, wouldn't we?" Julia eyed her friend with suspicion. Did Rachel hit her on the head at the turning in the hall and try to make it appear as though she only found her? Julia sat down on the bed near the copper piece.

"Then tell me about your cousin. Mr. Hunk with the spaniel eyes isn't Lord Maltby, is he? So where does that leave the great love of your life?"

Julia was caught off guard and at a total loss for an answer. There was a lot of water under the bridge since she so naively professed her love for her cousin, Nigel. Now the whole thing was absurd--laughable.

"You're right, Mr. Hunk is not Lord Maltby," she said, careful not to elaborate for fear of giving away Hampton's secrets. She buttered the toast and stuffed a piece in her mouth.

"Why all the mystery? I thought Nigel invited you here because he wanted to see you." Rachel waited for a response. When she got none she shrugged. "Well he's seen you all right. When you're in his presence, nothing could pry his eyes from you."

"How do you know which one he is?" Julia asked, her eyes bright with disbelief.

"It's pretty obvious who's boss around here, isn't it? Spaniel eyes, Mr. What's-his-name, isn't nearly as well educated as cousin Nigel, nor as well bred either. Besides, as you said when you arrived, he doesn't look anything like a Maltby. I've studied the photographs around the place very carefully. There's a photo of Nigel in the armor room, 'Lord Maltby swinging the mace to perfection,' it's titled."

"You've certainly been busy tending to *my* business." Julia didn't try to hide her annoyance. "Paul Hampton is the other man's real name. He's a private eye solving some problems for Nigel. Maybe they should make a detective of you. Perhaps you, like John Eldred, could solve all these problems in no time at all."

"Please...don't liken me to that nerd," Rachel whined. "I didn't know Professor Quayle, and I really can't get very upset about the murder. All I know about it is that I didn't have anything to do with it, and I think it's about time for us to leave...for your sake. I talked with Spaniel Eyes this afternoon. If the investigation goes well he said I can probably go home on time after all. Isn't that grand?"

Rachel looked down, picked at her nails for a minute, then dropped the bombshell. "The only problem now is that he says *you're* a prime suspect. What were you doing in that dark sculpture gallery alone the other night, hon?"

Julia's mouth hung open. "I was touring the castle."

Where did Paul Hampton get off telling everyone what he knew about her when he had nearly forced her to swear to secrecy about his and Nigel's plot? She frowned and studied Rachel's face for motive for this conversation. There was a vague wavering light at the end of a long dark tunnel. Twisting and twanging vibrations shifted and stalled, not quite coming into focus.

"Someone is deceiving me," Julia said, surprised at her sudden realization of it. Why is Rachel cleared by Paul Hampton so suddenly? Everyone was getting a different story. On the other hand, maybe Nigel and Paul Hampton were trying to flush Rachel out by lying to her. Who could guess what those two plotted.

"I have no idea who's deceiving whom," Rachel said with a lazy openmouthed yawn, "but I hope you can get it straightened out by plane time day after tomorrow. By the way, when are we going to have a look at the jewelry?"

"Why ask me?" Julia said faintly.

"Who else would I ask?"

Rachel banged herself on the side of the head with the flat of her hand like she was clearing her brain. "Control tower. Control tower. Come in, please," she called into a fist doubled into a pretend microphone. "Have lost my way. Please advise as to relationships, rationality, purpose, and possible outcome. Over." She took on a shocked expression with raised eyebrows as she listened for a time, then playfully hung up the mike. "The operator says I'm receiving information on the wrong wave length, that there are dark sinister happenings of which I am unaware. That makes sense in the light of the strange things that have gone on around here."

In spite of herself, Julia giggled. Rachel was the only person she knew who could make light of the worst possible scenario. If she could only ask her about the FBI and Jeremy Andrews. But if what Paul Hampton and Nigel told her about Rachel was true, and Rachel knew Julia was aware of it, would she try to kill her here and now when she was a long way from help? Again Julia weighed the advantages of the copper pot.

She nearly fainted with relief when Rachel stood up and headed for the door.

"I guess I never cared much for mysteries. My life is one of those boring 'open books' people occasionally own up to," Rachel said with regret. She turned at the door and smiled sympathetically. "Whatever it is, hon, I hope you get it squared away to your satisfaction. I came on this trip with a bubbling happy girl. I don't want to take home some sour old woman in her place. See you at breakfast." She closed the door softly.

Julia stared after her. Rachel had a lot of nerve spying on her like this. She obviously came to find out how much Julia could remember, whether she saw anything of the person who attacked her. When she found out Julia didn't know who had sneaked up behind her in the hall, Rachel was satisfied and left.

Julia finished her tea, then locked the door. She must try to get some sleep. Her days were filled with tension and she was not sleeping well. No telling what tomorrow might bring.

Chapter 23

Mae Eldred awoke earlier than usual. It was not quite dawn. The massive purple brocade draperies sprinkled with yellow chrysanthemums and stitched green leaves swayed rhythmically, like a charmed snake, to a gentle ocean breeze. She was nearly lulled back to a dreaming state by their hypnotic motion, but she forced herself awake. The niggling knowledge of the secret stairwell would not allow her to rest. She sat up in bed and studied John. His mouth hung open and he wheezed and snorted the hollow apnea-prone snores of the heavy drinker. He would be out for at least another two hours.

She threw her legs over the edge of the high French bed and slid to the floor. Laid out on a bedside chair were white polyester pants and a white sweatshirt. Matching white sox and walking shoes were all the needs she anticipated for her morning's adventure. She dressed and went to the bathroom and brushed her teeth as quietly as possible.

She brought her dyed-brown wiry curls under control with a few brush strokes. Her heart raced, pounded in her ears like a jackhammer. She opened the door and peered down the hall. The candles that were lit the evening before were now dark, and hazy shafts of morning light filtered through the tall arrow slits. A queasy odor of burned beeswax was heavy in the air. She switched on her flashlight and strode confidently down the dark passage.

The morning was as quiet as a graveyard. She hurried by Julia's door. Abruptly she stopped. There were voices coming from the room. Yes, definitely a man's voice. She listened. Thick walls and a heavy oak door made it impossible to make out conversation or recognize voices. She shrugged. No telling what the young women could get up to these days.

She hurried on. At the turning in the hall a coffee pot steamed on a small shelf in a niche in the wall. Sugar and cream pots covered with beaded lace, as well as a pink china plate heaped with crusty croissants sat near it. She paused momentarily, savoring the aroma of rich fresh coffee, wanting in the worst way to take a cup along, but she decided against it. Odors often gave one away.

She wanted nothing to deter her from her mission of covertly exploring the mysterious stairwell. It would be like the old days during the war, wouldn't it? Secretive and steeped in fear?

She and John worked as a team for the underground when they were young teenagers, pledged to be responsible for each other. One often had to stand by and watch the other walk headlong into circumstances that were, on occasion, life threatening. Perhaps that was why John became so protective. But could an intelligent woman allow her husband to know everything for both of them? *You can talk to me, I'll answer for both of us,* he told Walpole. The thought was unbearable. She simply could stand it no longer. She even hoped when John awoke he might be delirious with fear and jealousy at her absence. She chuckled. He would probably think she was gone to be with another man. How delightful it would be if he sought to blame it on Jeremy Andrews. She shook her head to clear it. Why was she thinking such silly thoughts?

She nearly ran down the main staircase. Her printed schedule said that breakfast would be served in an area other than the main dining room, so there was no need to worry about running into servants. She entered the dining room, but did not turn on her flashlight for fear it might draw attention. Heavy stained-glass windows kept out any trace of morning light.

She paused to accustom her eyes to the darkness. Lingering food odors from last night's dinner hung about the room. She moved forward cautiously, slowly thrusting each leg out in front of her to keep from running over a ginger jar or injuring herself on some spiked medieval doodad sticking prominently into the room.

When she got to the dining table she had no trouble finding the armoire. She hesitated for a moment over what she was about to do, then she calmly unlatched the cabinet door and stepped inside, quietly closing the door behind her. A bitterly cold draft swirled around her from somewhere above.

The flashlight swept over steep worn steps hewn between rough stone walls. She climbed quickly, pausing now and again to listen, for what, she was not sure. She soon came to a landing, turned a forty-five degree angle, and climbed again.

At the top she paused and peered through a narrow door that opened onto a long high-roofed hall with an enormous divided-pane window in the opposite end, looking like the distant end of a railway tunnel, for only a feather-light touch of dawn teased the window. The air was saturated with the odors of disuse, and loose rolls of witches' hair skittered in dusty gray clouds around her feet as she moved. She had climbed at least four levels and now crossed over the orangery through a thick stone passage that separated the keep from the unrestored portion of the castle.

Reluctantly she turned to look behind her. Could she find her way back to the dining room?

Chapter 24

She slept fitfully, but now she was jolted awake, listening. It was a faraway sound, but it was enough to wake her. It dragged Julia from the menacing arms of a faceless stranger who intended to do her some unnamed harm to finding herself standing up in bed, perspiring from the frightening dream, and at the same time shivering from the cold. Dreamy cobwebs began to recede, clearing her brain, and she scrunched down among the pillows, taking comfort from her grandmother's familiar room.

It came again. An insistent businesslike rap on the door. The sound brought her leaping from the high bed wide-eyed with fear. A suggestion of dawn played at the windows. She pulled on a fuzzy blue robe and tiptoed to the door.

"Who is it?" she asked quietly.

"It's Walpole, Miss. I've got the pictures."

Did he have to shout it through the castle? Julia fumbled with the lock and got the door open before he had a chance to shout again. Walpole peered at her from the darkness like a ferret coming out of a hole.

"Just a minute. Let me get the light," Julia whispered. She glanced at the bedside clock. It was eight a.m.

An odor of tobacco preceded Walpole into the room. His blue eyes swept over her fitted robe and lingered on her tousled hair. "I saw to it that the blokes at the camera shop got them done in jig time, just as you

142

requested, Miss." He handed her a sealed Kodak envelope. "I 'ope you'll 'ave a very nice party."

"Thank you, Inspector," Julia smiled sweetly. "And remember, not a word to anyone." She was grossly unfair to the poor man. She got her purse from the dressing table drawer. "Now, what do I owe you?"

"Consider it a favor, Miss," he said, contemplating her eyes and mouth. "Sorry about your 'ead. Mr. 'ampton filled me in about your accident. After a few errands this morning I intend to remain on the premises and give the case my full attention 'til the whole thing is solved. We can't tolerate any more dangerous rousting about, eh?"

"Do you know yet who murdered Professor Quayle?" It happened only four days ago, but it seemed like an eternity.

"Not yet, but I have an idea. One 'as to be sure."

"Are you going to blame me?" she asked, flinching inside.

Walpole's eyes twinkled. "Did you do it?"

"Of course not."

"Do you know who did?"

"Wouldn't I say?"

"We'll see then." His eyes returned again and again to the envelope Julia held. She could see that he wanted her to open it. He was a suspicious man. She watched him amble about the room, taking in the jeans, sweater, and a pair of no-nonsense square-toed walking shoes she laid out for the day.

He stopped abruptly, like he had been bitten, and gave a skeptical perusal of the beauty paraphernalia that littered the dresser top--makeup, perfumes, combs and brushes, face creams and powders--as though they were alive and prepared to snare a poor unsuspecting male as he passed. He may have thought of himself as inured to these female ways, but Julia knew better.

She interrupted his thoughts by walking to the door and opening it for him. She thanked him again for his trouble and waited for him to leave.

He glanced longingly at the unopened envelope in her hand. "Did you want to make sure the pictures turned out nicely? They don't always come out well, do they?"

143

"I'm sure they'll be perfectly adequate," Julia said, somewhat breathlessly. Why didn't he leave? What was he waiting for? Her hands shook uncontrollably by the time she got the door closed behind him.

She went straight to the lamp and ripped open the envelope. A box of slides fell onto the table. She removed them from the box and stacked them neatly, postponing as long as possible her inevitable meeting with the curious unknown.

The last of the frames, marked number twenty-four, was on top. It was black. She picked up the others in turn and found them all to be black until she came to number nine. She could see before she held it to the light that it had something on it. She gasped in horror as she stared, open mouthed, at the image.

Paul Hampton stood in front of Nigel's open safe with a packet of papers in his hand. His eyes were wide with surprise and glowed red from the flashbulb, giving them a primitive savage look. His mouth was drawn down in an angry grimace as he glared viciously into the camera.

"Oh, my God," she said, dropping like a deflated balloon onto the red velvet chair. A tumbled mosaic of lies and treachery orbited before her eyes, and yet, she could not quite relate all of its elements. "Oh, my God," she said again out loud. "Poor Professor Quayle. He must have taken this photograph." She knew what she must do. She must warn Nigel before anything else unsavory could happen.

She jumped from the chair, scooped the rest of the slides into the drawer of the night stand, and pulled on jeans and a heavy rag wool sweater. While trying to pull on knee socks, she fell heavily on the rug. She scrambled up again. Nothing could hurt her now. She must find Nigel. Her hands trembled so violently that her shoelaces tangled into a hopeless knot. She left them flapping.

She grabbed up the slide and ran through the hall and down the wide dark staircase that led to the massive front doors. A heavy chain-like gate with a thick surly black padlock fortified it. She shook the gate in frustration, sending a barrage of staccato artillery-like echoes rattling through the castle. Why did she come this way? She should have gone through the garden.

"Can I help?" a voice behind her asked. "I was just on my way to see you. You've come to warn Lord Maltby, is that it, Luv?"

How did he know what she was about? Did he have her room bugged? Julia shoved the slide deep into her pocket and whirled around to face Paul Hampton. She watched his quick glance take in her uncombed hair, an unzipped fly on her jeans, and tangled shoelaces. At the same time, her peripheral vision caught sight of a moving white cap at the end of the hall near the morning room where preparations for breakfast were underway. A servant's hall nearly caused her death once. Now she hoped it might save her.

She had never considered taking up acting as a career, as her father suggested, but lately she was beginning to understand that there was some merit to it. She gazed hazily at Hampton, then put both hands over her face as though to wipe away a cobweb.

"Oh," she moaned loudly, shaking her head in distress. "Oh, I'm so glad you're here. I...I was having a nightmare. The enemy was at the gate." It was an old line her father relied on many a time in a pinch when botched lines in a play needed reviving. He always said it could mean anything. Where did it come from, she wondered, undocumented folklore? The Bible? Why was she thinking about it?

"I was supposed to make it fast against the crowd. We were all going to die a horrible death." An avalanche of tears came easily. More than from acting, they came from sheer fright. She pretended to try again to clear her head, when, in the background, sweet and clear, she heard the servant's voice.

"Mr. 'ampton," the girl said politely, approaching them from behind. "Lord Maltby is waiting to see you in 'is office." Her mouth dropped open as she stared questioningly at Julia's disarray and Paul Hampton's obvious frustration.

Julia's eyes never left Hampton's face. It was full of cunning. She could see him weighing the possibilities as he gaped at the girl.

He turned back to Julia, studying her face as if he were not quite sure what she was up to. He spoke over his shoulder. "Tell Lord Maltby he's needed in Miss Maltby's room straightaway."

"Yes, sir."

"Miss Maltby, you should be in bed. That medication has made you stark raving mad," Hampton said in a loud voice the servant could hear. His arm shot out and gripped Julia tightly around the waist while he hurried her up the staircase, each of them stumbling over the other's feet.

Julia flinched at his touch. He was going to take her upstairs, wait for Nigel, then kill them both. She tried to twist from his grasp, but his clench held her in a viselike grip.

Chapter 25

The servant had done her duty. Paul Hampton barely reached the top step with Julia in tow when Nigel bounded up behind them, taking three steps at a time.

"What is this? What's wrong, Julia?"

"I'm afraid the medication has made our girl have nightmares," Hampton said huskily. He gave Julia's arm a painful pinch, which she supposed was meant to keep her quiet. "I found her sleepwalking downstairs, trying to make sure Gorlachen's gates are secure."

Nigel laughed with delight. "Gorlachen's gates have been secure for centuries, Julia. It certainly would surprise me if someone tried to get through them now."

Hampton forced an agreeable laugh, while in a halfhearted manner he helped Nigel get Julia to bed. It was no surprise to her when he suddenly disappeared.

"Where did he go?" she asked, peering cautiously around Nigel, who was trying his best to make her comfortable.

"He has a meeting with Walpole in my office." He stopped fussing with her clothes, pulled back, and eyed her skeptically. "One would think you bloody well can't get on without him. What's going on here anyway?"

Julia put her finger to her lips in an urgent plea for silence. She picked up a pen and writing pad from the bedside table and wrote a note: *This room is bugged. Let's find it quickly, then we can talk.*

Nigel laughed uneasily and avoided her eyes by picking at a loose yarn on his black-and-white tweed sweater.

Julia covered his hand with hers to force him to look at her. He jumped slightly at her unexpected touch. "I didn't know you cared." He grinned boyishly, but the grin quickly vanished when Julia fixed wide eyes darkly formidable with terror on his.

In one swift glance he got the message. He strode to the stained glass lampshade and ran his hand around the lower rim. Out came a small plastic device which he smashed underfoot.

Julia watched him, confused. Was he in on it? Was he going to finish off some preconceived plan between himself and Paul Hampton? She must take the chance.

"Did you have my room bugged at Paul Hampton's request?" The idea was bitter as gall and nearly choked off her voice.

Nigel's face flushed darkly. "You have to understand the position all these goings-on have put me in, Julia. You come here bringing with you a woman who has been closely watched by the FBI in the States. Then we find she's married to a man who is here, on these same premises, posing brazenly as someone else. What was I to do?"

"I would certainly hate to catch a person posing brazenly as someone else." Her voice dripped with sarcasm. "Besides, it's all a lie." She sat very still and watched a totally blank expression cross his face.

"I don't know what you mean." His skin flushed a deep purple, as though he were finding it difficult to control his temper. "I've run myself to death and gone to a great deal of expense to make sure you remain safe while you're here. The least you can do for me is overlook...."

"Falling rocks and a nearly terminal clout on the head?" Her biting sarcasm stopped him. "Look at this." She reached out to him with the slide.

He drew back from the object as though it that might strike him. "What is it?"

"Look for yourself." Was Walpole keeping Hampton busy, or did he escape to some dark secret room of the castle hoping to hear their conversation?

Nigel's arm was locked in place in the glow of the lamp as he studied the slide interminably. The deep flush drained from his face.

"Do you believe me now?" Julia asked softly.

"Where did you get this?"

"It's a long story, but first I think you should find Walpole and make sure Paul Hampton is kept very busy until we decide what to do. You see, he knows I have the slide. I guess you told Professor Quayle your real identity and my relationship to you."

"Yes, he knew me. He has written about Gorlachen several times. He was willing to keep the secret."

Julia nodded. "I think Professor Quayle was abducted from this room while he waited for me to return from my tour of the castle in quest of the branding irons that first night. Before Hampton got to him, Quayle came to find me. When I wasn't here, he stuffed the film with the picture of Hampton robbing the safe in the toe of my shoe where he knew I would eventually find it and give it to you. I can't tell you how many times Hampton has taken this room apart looking for that film. I tricked Inspector Walpole into having it developed for me. Of course, I had no idea what was on it. Now I realize I was the only person with the answer."

While Julia talked, she brushed her hair, tied her shoelaces, and tidied her clothes.

Nigel could not speak. Time and again he put the slide up to the light and examined its contents. Then, as though the full meaning of their predicament finally struck home, he buried the slide deep in his trouser's pocket and grabbed Julia's hand. "He'll be back. Let's get out of here."

They fled hand in hand, down the hazy gray back passage, like the very devil was in pursuit, their shoes making dull echoing thuds on the smoothly worn stone floor. Julia thought it sounded like a dozen people running after them.

"Quit looking back, Julia, you'll fall."

"Someone's coming," she cried.

"It's only an echo. Keep moving."

They raced breathlessly past the magic cello and down the steep and uneven steps that Julia negotiated alone in her search for the branding irons. Dangerous people were far more frightening than the dark. They came to a crossing and Nigel hurried through his office door marked "Private." Walpole and Hampton were gone.

"Bloody hell," Nigel said.

The same dark-eyed servant, Julia's angel of mercy, came whipping up the hall, her starched uniform swinging in rhythm with her purposeful step. "Inspector Walpole said he must return to the mainland for a spell this morning, Lord Maltby. He left Mr. 'ampton in charge," she said efficiently.

"Where is Hampton?" Nigel asked. A menacing quality in his voice smacked of resolute fury.

"I don't know sir," she responded, suddenly gone timid. She looked from Nigel to Julia, realizing something of grave importance was going on and wondering whether she was to blame.

"Keep the servants in the kitchen until you're told otherwise, will you please, Rose?"

"Yes, sir," she said, her sleepy eyes suddenly alert.

Julia watched with intense interest as Nigel picked up his intercom. "Lewis, activate all surveillance. Let the dogs out to patrol the walls, and warn all guests to stay in their rooms with the doors locked. Keep an eye out for Paul Hampton. I don't want him to leave the premises."

He turned to Julia. "Let's find the room he's recording in." He reached in a lower desk drawer, pulled out a knife, and stuck it in his belt. From the wall behind a polished Chippendale writing table he took a four-inch mace with a three-foot nylon rope attached.

"What are you going to do with that?" She remembered what Rachel told her about his photograph in the armory.

"You came for a medieval good time, did you not? Maybe you'll see a little brutal retribution this morning."

"But...but why not call in the police? They're paid to do this kind of thing," she said, agonizing over the ugly sight of the mace.

"Walpole *is* police," he said. "So far he's been totally ineffective. Besides, nobody knows this castle like I do. I have the advantage of having played hide-and-seek for years about the place. There isn't a niche or cranny where Hampton can hide from me."

His dreadful calm alarmed Julia, but she was beginning to understand. Her cousin was steeped in the medieval. He studied and relived the ancient ways throughout his childhood. The scar of the Celtic cross was part of it. Now he had a chance to make more of it a reality. She shrank from the horrifying weapon he held. Her only encounter with the likes of an armor-cracking mace was in the pretend swinging of it her father resorted to. She met Nigel's eyes and knew he recognized the distaste she felt for what he was about to do.

"I take it you're not finding this experience particularly edifying," he said, his eyes leaving hers fleetingly, then moving back to bore into them.

"Sorry." Julia smarted under his scrutiny. She must summon the strength to help him stop Hampton. His harmonious castle life was invaded. She had the distinct feeling that his real anger was with himself for having been sucked into the devious plot.

In spite of how she tried to concentrate on the problem at hand, she simply could not help but think how thoroughly aggravated Rachel was going to be when she found out what she missed this morning. *Rachel*, she thought helplessly. She was treating her good friend so shabbily. How could she ever make it up to her?

Nigel barred the office door on the inside. Julia thought that perhaps they were simply going to sit and wait for Paul Hampton to break the door down. A miserable image came to mind of Paul Hampton splintering the door with some vicious-looking pointed medieval instrument, while Nigel stood ready, swinging the mace in rhythmic motion to crush Hampton's skull like an eggshell when he entered the room.

Fascinated, Julia watched Nigel cross the room to a full-length portrait of their grandfather. He pulled it away from the wall on balky hinges, revealing a low narrow door that led into a black hole. Julia peered into it. "What is *that*?" she asked while she wrinkled her nose at the heady odor of disuse wafting from it.

"It leads into the castle's hidden escape tunnels," he explained. "Come on. A little dirt won't hurt you. Let's get this over with."

They entered the stone passage and he pulled the door shut behind them. Dust clotted the dead-cold air.

"Don't cough and don't speak," he said. "Every sound carries."

151

Chapter 26

Paul Hampton scrambled up four flights of steep oak steps in the closed wing of the castle to get to the sculpture storage room. Unlike the parts of the fortress open to the public, this section of some forty-two rooms was built in the fourteenth century and was isolated from the keep by a Herculean orangery built between them.

Although the unrestored section was in a poor state of repair, it was not as old as the keep. Unlike stone-vaulted corridors within thick walls, these halls were sagging, complaining oak timbers running through the center of the structure. There was a fuggy odor of neglect, of things secret and long forgotten. Much of the woodwork curled loose from the frames. Dust and spider webs enshrouded the halls like tacky gray felt. It was obvious that there was not much happening here anymore.

Hampton peered inside the room. The stored Italian sculptures were, themselves, priceless, crowded together like folks at a busy bus stop, and seemed to study him with their wide hollow eyes like they questioned his authority to be there. He jumped back. Did one of them move? His eyes searched the room. Satisfied that no one was waiting for him, he stepped inside and closed the heavy door. He ran across the room to the recorder, scattering loose dust and other detritus in his wake.

A hard knot formed in his stomach when there was nothing on the tape but the beginning of Julia and Nigel's conversation. It was over. He might have been gone by now if it wasn't for that bloody professor and his film, and the maid who interfered with his taking Julia to her room this morning. He could have settled the whole score by getting rid of Julia right then, destroying the slide, and letting Rachel Givens and Jeremy Andrews take the fall. It could have worked long enough for him to pocket the cash he found in the safe, then take off for the States. He pulled a Continental airline ticket for a late afternoon flight from his case. He bought it under the name of Hugh Brooks. If only he could get off the castle grounds and make that flight.

He hurriedly latched the recorder's case, shoved it out of sight under the covers of two of the larger sculptures, then entered the hall to look for a way out without having to go down the main staircase. He rushed to the high window at the end of the long corridor and peered out to see what the possibilties were. A sheer stone wall dropped four levels to the roiling North Sea.

He turned the knob of the nearest door and entered the room to check out any windows he might escape through. It was stacked with old trunks and assorted luggage and smelled of mouse droppings and moldy leather. A filthy cobwebby window, too small for a man to crawl through, let in a narrow shaft of opaque morning light.

How did he get himself into this position? It was a snap decision on his part, a foolish decision, although the idea of it lurked on a subconscious level for years. With each new detective job he took in an important house the idea grew more prominent, more irresistible. He remembered all too well the moment he made the decision to carry it through.

Nigel Maltby chose Hampton for his detective skills on a referral from one of Hampton's former clients. Nigel handed him the guest list. *"There is a young woman on that list named Rachel Givens, a gemologist from New York City coming to Gorlachen with my cousin, Julia Maltby. Since Julia and I must decide on the ownership of priceless jewelry, I'm curious about Givens. Why would Julia be bringing a gemologist to Gorlachen? Can you check her out for me?"*

"Leave it to me, sir. I'll take care of it right away."

Nigel didn't elaborate further, but Hampton figured the jewelry had belonged to the crown at one time or another. At least that was what the important families all claimed. From Nigel's instructions and declaration of trust, it was so easy. It was as if the whole plan was jerked from his

153

mind and placed in the hands of another, one who took it over and left him totally unable to resist. Nigel was a congenial, paranoid sort, ready to believe anything he was told about the safety of his assets. Hampton planned to take the jewelry, money, and whatever valuables he could get his hands on and leave the country. Once he started to plan it, reasonable workable lies came in irresistible waves.

"It's a good thing we checked," Hampton cheerfully lied to Nigel. *"Rachel Givens has been implicated in several jewelry heists in the States. The FBI has had her under surveillance more than once."*

It only made good sense to implicate young Andrews, a single computer analyst listed on the roster also hailing from New York City. It was almost too easy to fit him into the plot-- *"There's another guest on your list you'd better look out for, sir. One Jeremy Andrews, also from New York City. Your gemologist, Rachel Givens, is secretly married to him. What do you suppose the two of them have up their sleeves?"* Implicating Andrews gave the whole story a certain knotty twist that rang plausible to Nigel's ears. His eyes were wide with the fear of treachery.

"What am I to do about it?" Nigel asked eagerly.

From that simple inquiry he and Nigel plotted the identity switch to allow Hampton the run of the castle--and, hopefully, to allow for Hampton to blame Rachel and Andrews when certain items of great value disappeared.

The deception planted a seed of doubt in Nigel's mind about his dear cousin, Julia, too--a reason to wonder why she kept such questionable company. Little did Hampton realize the dividends of Julia's suspecting Nigel as well. It could have been so perfect....

Then things started to go wrong. When he learned that Julia and Nigel were to visit Dunrose Manor, he entered the house through the back stairs and hid upstairs to hear their conversation, hopefully to learn where the jewels were kept. A squeaky floor gave him away and he had to escape without the information he was looking for. Then there was Quayle. He had the run of the castle to take photographs for his book and caught Hampton red-handed in the safe. He snapped the picture then disappeared with the film. Hampton finally ran him down in Julia's

154

room, but he didn't count on murder as part of the bargain. Bloody hell... murder! Even after a severe beating Quayle had no intention of telling him where the film was hidden. A little reasoning left him with the thought that Quayle left it in Julia's room so she would give it to Nigel.

Dear cousin Julia was about as sweet as a mating badger in springtime. When Hampton happened on her secret tour of the castle the night he killed Quayle, he followed her. What a treat it was to find her shoe buckle in the long-forgotten sculpture gallery. It was an excellent idea to move Quayle's body near it to keep Julia dangling as a major suspect.

Oh, God, it might have been so perfect. After missing Julia with the falling rock at the abbey, why in bloody hell couldn't he have hit her more squarely when he had his chance in the back hall? The episode replayed before his eyes....

Clickety-clack, clickety-clack, the ridiculously high heels came toward him from somewhere in the corridor. Julia sauntered down the hall with a slight smile on her face, looking as though she had not a care in the world. He watched her turn her back to him and place the cello in the cradle. When the time was right he jumped from his hiding place in the dark hallway and struck her a hard lick on the head. Bam! Down she went just like he planned. He watched a pool of blood form beneath her head. Was she dead? He stared helplessly at her body. Then she began to move and he was about to hit her again when he heard more clacketing heels coming toward him in one of the intersecting hallways. He became frightened and retreated to an alcove behind him where he could watch the goings-on.....

He shuddered to think of his behavior. Rachel's piercing screams on finding Julia echoed through his head.

He shook his head to clear it of images that were getting him nowhere. He was not going to be safe anywhere inside the castle. Nigel would sniff him out like a bloodhound. Hampton saw the photographs of the Lord of Gorlachen in the armory on the ground floor when he took his first tour of the castle, row upon row of photographs of Nigel demonstrating the use of the mace, the sword, the lance. He not only collected medieval instruments, they lived in his hands like live cunning vipers. Such moneyed men had power and advantages the average man never dreamed of.

Hampton shuddered again, gazed around him, and wiped perspiration from his face.

He was doing himself no good here. A squeak in the floor somewhere in the corridor jerked him around with a sudden desperate fear. Did Nigel find him already? He took a small revolver from his belt and cracked the door of the trunk room. He gaped dumbly at the figure coming down the hall.

Mae Eldred sauntered lightly down the passage, stopping occasionally in what appeared to be a contemplation of the noisy squeaks her steps made. She looked into rooms at random, then continued her trip down the hall, touching marble busts, intricately-carved tables, and other art objects placed in niches along the walls. She ran her hand slowly around the smooth cold interior of a multicolored ancient porcelain jar as though taking in its history through her touch. She hummed Saint-Saens' "The Swan" as she went. Her voice was charmingly high and clear.

The tune had gone round and round in Hampton's head until it nearly drove him crazy ever since the Maltby girl's solo. He thought this morning that perhaps he was rid of it, and here was Mae Eldred of all people bringing it back to haunt him. He watched her sit down on the threadbare cushion of an ornately-carved high-backed Spanish chair. It was oversized and resembled a throne. She smiled happily as she sat there swinging her legs, as though daydreaming of the luxurious lives of kings and queens.

Hampton was nailed to the floor. What in bloody hell was Mae Eldred doing in this part of the castle? She obviously was not looking for him. She didn't look as though she expected to run into anyone.

She left the chair and moved in his direction. He carefully closed the door. He held his breath and leaned heavily against the doorknob as her steps came closer. He felt the pressure of her hand trying to turn the knob, but his weight against it discouraged her and she turned to another door nearby. Apparently she was not impressed with the room's contents, for she sniffed unpleasantly and quickly moved on. She began to hum the Saint Seans' tune again from the beginning, the tones getting lighter and clearer as her lilting voice soared up the scale.

He could not decide what to do. There was no reason to harm Mae Eldred. She was simply a bored late middle-aged matron enjoying a secret morning's escape from her boorish husband. Hampton felt sorry for the woman from the beginning. She tolerated the old sot better than most would. He stayed where he was for several minutes, then cracked the door again to look down the hall. She was out of sight. She was moving down one of the adjoining corridors. He listened for a time. The floor creaked again some distance away.

He moved deftly into the hall and examined narrow double doors that appeared to close in a linen closet. Inside there were floor-to-ceiling shelves on either side of the door with a walk between. Hampton found himself confronted by a shaft of light visible through a razor-thin slit across the wall. He probed it with his fingers. In the midst of a great cloud of dust a shoddily-crafted door, scarcely large enough for a man to crawl through, fell open. He grinned.

Past experience from working with wealthy titled families in big country houses and castles taught him that the owners were often paranoid about the safety of both themselves and their possessions. He had seen many hidden rooms and secret passages camouflaged in a similar manner. Indeed, it was often one of the first things the owners proudly showed him upon his arrival on a new job, although Nigel wasn't among them. Most of the passages were built centuries ago when the buildings were fortified, but the modern families took great pride in them, both as a source of curiosity, and a far-fetched belief that they might be of significant use some day.

The secret door's hinges were wisely hidden by the shelf uprights. Mae Eldred probably would never notice them if she happened to open the closet doors. Hampton slipped into the escape tunnel and pulled the door to. There was barely space to stand up comfortably. A tiny skylight let in a wisp of gray light over his head. He turned on a flashlight and directed the beam down the darkness of the chute.

The floor dropped steadily and sharply down hill to the interior of

157

the castle. As it dropped, the roof gained more height. It was as though the passage was an afterthought and crammed into whatever space was available after the initial building process. He turned off the light. He could not risk giving himself away.

The further he crept from the skylight the bleaker the tunnel became. He cried out in surprise when he stumbled over two steps, painfully wrenching his ankle. He turned on the flashlight to examine the location. He stood on what appeared to be a landing.

Thwack. The sound came from somewhere below him accompanied by a draft of stale cold air. Someone, somewhere, entered the tunnel. He heard agitated whispers, then silence.

He shook so hard he could scarcely switch off the light. The darkness disoriented him. He was descending, but he could not fathom how far he was from the linen closet or on which level he was. The tunnel curved slightly and he could no longer see the tiny skylight. In frustration and panic he groped along the wall until he felt the unmistakable crack of another entry. He pushed against the crack with all his strength. The trap door fell open and landed with a thud on a familiar carpet.

Chapter 27

Julia obediently stumbled along in solid darkness behind Nigel, feeling her way up and down uneven steps and crawling through filthy trapdoors. She was disgusted, cold, and miserable. The tunnel had the consistency and odor of cheap dark wine floating in a silent dust storm. Her nose stopped up and her sinuses ached.

"Are we breathing Norman air?" she asked. She felt Nigel's body tense as he stopped in his tracks with an unmistakable sigh of impatience.

"I have been asked a lot of dumb questions about this castle, such as "Do these suits of armor come in standard sizes? or 'What are we lookin' at here?' or 'Who was Norman?' and 'Why would the Scots want to capture an isolated down-at-the-heels place like this?' all asked by uninformed American tourists, but you take the cake, Julia. Try thinking about the fact that you're a Maltby and about the problem at hand instead of how uncomfortable the castle is, please."

Julia was beyond caring what he thought about her analysis of the place. "What are you going to do?" she whispered into the darkness.

"Hush."

"I will not hush. I will not stand by and watch you torment a man with cruel and inhuman weapons. I'm going back to my room. I won't be a party to it."

"You'll stay with me," he said harshly. He clamped a steely cold hand on her arm. "You're my responsibility, and I don't intend to let you out of my sight again until your 'Mr. Charming' is caught. You won't find him very charming if he happens to have a gun in his hand. Besides, I wasn't going to kill him anyway." He was standing perfectly still now, as though deep in thought.

For a fleeting moment Nigel was transported to the past. He was growing up and losing interest in medieval games. He had even come to fear them a little. One evening his father dared him to travel through the maze of secret dark passages from one end of the castle to the other, and from top to bottom one last time. He even set up a straw man for him-- the Scots were storming the gate. Nigel's job was to warn all areas of the castle, and move the inhabitants to safety in the keep. He made a perfect trip through the entire web of escape tunnels in total darkness, and came out through the armoire in the dining room where his father waited for him. He was twelve years old at the time. That was sixteen years ago. He hadn't been through the escape tunnels since. He wondered now if he remembered.

Even while his thoughts tumbled over and over through the past, Nigel was aware of the warning thud of a trap door opening, then closing quietly up ahead. It was enough years ago since he maneuvered the doors that he could not be sure from which level the sound came. A gut reaction told him it was level four. He used to recognize the peculiarities of each door instantly, like the sound of one's own automobile engine, or a wheezy sewing machine insisting on its own way. How in God's name did Hampton find the escape tunnel?

"We'll have to go back," he said, disappointment choking his voice. "He knows we're here."

"I...I'm sorry," Julia whispered. "I didn't mean to give us away."

"It wasn't your fault. He was probably in the tunnel when we entered it. He's on level four, so we'll leave on three. He won't have any more luck finding us than we'll have finding him. Do be quiet and keep your eyes and ears open."

He took her hand while he groped for the next trapdoor. Her hand was small and cold in his. He held it tightly. Beyond everything, he wanted her to be safe and warm.

"What are we going to do now?" she asked, breaking into his thoughts.

160

"We're going back to the keep and let Hampton come to us. He really has no place to go. There is no point in chasing him through forty-two rooms and in and out of this tunnel all day. We'll let Walpole handle it when he gets back from the mainland. A pair of dogs will get the job done."

Nigel thought it must be the most reasonable thing to do. If the secret tunnel was not as well camouflaged as he thought he remembered from those many years ago, then perhaps his ability to protect Julia and himself was also questionable. He could not put Julia in danger. He had secretly loved her for years. He knew that now. She was finally with him at Gorlachen. He must not risk losing her.

"We'll go down the main stairwell. Let Hampton have the tunnel."

They crawled into daylight on the third level.

Julia was glad to step out of the dead chill into a musty oak-paneled room that had once been a very handsome library. There were collections of old books in tattered leather bindings piled in disorganized heaps on a dark red and gold threadbare Persian carpet. Piles of books lay hit and miss on floor-to-ceiling shelves. At the opposite end of the room, seventy feet away, was a roped-off dais in front of a massive blackened oak fireplace. Waxwork characters dressed in ancient seedy costumes were arranged in a conversational display before it. Queen Victoria and her beloved Albert stood in conjugal bliss near the hearth. Several others were seated in lifelike positions around them while another group was pushed out of the way in a jumble against the wall.

Julia gaped at the elegant shabbiness of a bygone era. "Why would you allow such a beautiful room to go to ruin like this?" she asked, saddened by its neglect.

"Money," Nigel said simply. "In the past few weeks I've come to grips with the fact that, as badly as I'd like to, I'm unable to support the renovation of the whole place. It might take several million pounds." He sorted through a stack of books. "Actually this is my favorite room in the entire castle. When I was a child, my father and I sat in front of that fireplace and read scary stories to each other. I have contacted Madame Tussaud's Gallery to come get their waxwork figures. Father allowed

161

them to be placed here for bed and breakfast guests to enjoy. As it turned out, we never got this far with the restoration, and I never liked the bloody things anyway. Too lifelike."

He placed his hands on his hips and surveyed the chaos of the room. "As you can see, I've been sorting the books, trying to categorize them in some reasonable way. If I can convince the National Trust the castle needs to be saved for posterity they'll refurbish it, save everything, and I can live here and enjoy it the rest of my life."

"Wouldn't you hate to lose control of it? I mean this castle has been a Maltby stronghold for generations. How can you possibly consider giving it up?" The thought of losing the lovely room caught at Julia's throat and renewed her new-found emotions of being an historical Maltby.

So strong was her sentiment at the moment that she completely forgot that Paul Hampton wanted to kill them. She was sharply reminded of it when Nigel ignored what she was saying and abruptly crossed the room and knelt down on the Persian rug.

"What is this?" he said, leaning over the rug to examine a dark stain.

Julia felt slightly ill as she watched him run his fingers through the spot. It was the size of a dinner plate--lumpy, dry, and quite stiff. Reddish-black flakes stuck to the ends of his fingers. He crossed the room to show her. "It's blood." A sudden awareness of death rattled him. "Hampton must have killed the professor in here, then moved his body to the sculpture gallery where he found your shoe buckle."

The instant Julia saw Nigel lean over the spot, a sudden sense of foreboding gripped her. The whole picture popped up before her, sharp and clear. Mae had, indeed, seen Hampton drag Professor Quayle away to be murdered. When Quayle would not give up the film, he signed his death warrant. Now she and Nigel were in immediate danger....

"Nigel..."

The words stuck in her throat as Nigel shouted, "Get down Julia!" He pushed her roughly to the floor behind a heavy mahogany writing desk.

Only as a blur on her peripheral vision did Julia see the character rise, like a quick jack-in-the-box, from the jumble of wax bodies heaped against the wall. Instantly two shots drilled Nigel's shouts like sharp nails through tin sheeting. The staccato cracks echoed eerily through the high-ceilinged room. Next came a cry of anguish, a heavy thud that shook the floor, and Nigel was hunched over her, cringing under the desk with his head down.

They turned to see Inspector Walpole in the door behind them, his legs spread stiffly apart, his gun held firmly in both hands while still pointed directly at Paul Hampton.

"We can't 'ave American ladies solving our murders for us now, can we? Our helpful Mr. 'ampton won't kill again," he said solemnly.

Abruptly two other police officers burst through the door. One knelt by Hampton to administer first aid.

Walpole, who appeared to be in shock, blinked in dismay as he looked from Nigel to Julia, then at Hampton adding more blood to the Persian carpet.

"I didn't go to the mainland this morning," he said. "It was too risky the way things 'ave been going. On a hunch I checked with the FBI yesterday. They 'ave no records on Rachel Givens or young Andrews. 'Ampton was just trying to cover his own behavior by casting doubts on the two New Yorkers."

"I can't believe this," Nigel said, shaking his head in wonder. "He seemed like such a reliable chap."

"He was too bloody 'andy at barging into situations after the fact," Walpole said. "One must always be on the lookout for behavior patterns."

A parade of servants peered nervously through the door.

"Get an ambulance for this man. He has a leg wound," Nigel said to one of them. Then he gripped Walpole's hand. "Good work, Walpole. You saved our bacon." He helped Julia up and brushed dust from her clothes and hair. "You okay? Bloody hell, I thought sure he was on the fourth level."

"There will be an investigation. All shootings, regardless of circumstances, are investigated," Walpole said.

"You can count on me for the best kind of support, Walpole," Nigel said. "The shooting was, in all of our judgments here, a necessity."

That settled, Walpole's watery blue gaze settled on Julia, taking in the disheveled blond hair dusted with webs, her dirt-smudged face, hands, and clothes. He frowned as though she were a long-dreamed-of wife who had suddenly disappointed her faithful husband by cheating him blind.

"It was something to do with the pictures, was it not, Miss?" he asked her, his slightly nasal voice betraying bitter disappointment that he was not privy to the important discovery.

"I'm afraid it was," Julia said. She regretted having used him so shamelessly.

He continued to frown at her for a moment, then collected himself and began to give orders to his lads. But suddenly, as though he had forgotten to bring out a Christmas gift that lay wrapped on the closet shelf for months, he jumped to a door camouflaged by a trompe l'oeil English garden and jerked it open.

"You can come out now, Mrs. Eldred," Walpole said rather pompously, as though he finally found a way to save face by having the last word.

Mae Eldred emerged from the closet with terror in her eyes, her hands held high over her head like a bank robber with a gun held to her head. "Oh, my bloody God," she said when she saw Paul Hampton sprawled in a lumpy heap on the floor. The terrified expression on her face, along with dust webs caught in frizzy curls, gave her the look of a chunk of petrified coconut. She peered at them accusingly, with mouth wide open, as though she thought they had shot and killed Lord Maltby and were now going to shoot her for having entered the hidden stairwell. A glance at Walpole's gun, which he still held rigidly at his side, was enough to send her into a fit of babbling hysteria.

"I hid in the armoire in the dining room, but it turned out to be a stairwell...I didn't bother anything, honest I didn't. I just wanted to see something John had never seen...I only walked up the hall and looked into the rooms...and I would never pinch anything...please...please don't shoot me," she begged, then fell into a fit of uncontrollable sobbing.

Nigel and Julia gawked blankly at each other, then at Walpole, then back at Mae.

"What in bloody hell is she doing up here?" Nigel asked.

"Mrs. Eldred was having 'erself a nice little stroll through the castle early this morning," Walpole said with a twinkle in his eye. "I discovered her when I came looking for 'ampton. When she heard me come down the hall she became frightened and ran into the library closet. I thought she'd be safe there so I left her alone. Then, indeed, to my astonishment, Mr. 'ampton popped out of that trapdoor over there. He dove into the waxworks bodies for cover when you two emerged from the same door in this same room, both of you strolling about in front of 'im as unconcerned as peacocks on the front lawn. He didn't try to get away because he knew I had 'im covered from the doorway."

Walpole blinked several times like he was trying to convince himself it all really happened that way. "I didn't know if 'ampton had a gun, but I couldn't allow a threat to your lives. You two are indeed lucky I got a clear shot at him when he jumped up to make a run for it. I can testify that Mrs. Eldred had nothing at all to do with it."

Julia watched helplessly while Nigel tried to comfort Mae, who was distraught to the point of near collapse.

"It's all right, my dear," he said, handing her a handkerchief. "Nothing has been hurt. Of course you did disobey the rules, but I think I can make allowances in this case."

Mae blew her nose, then gazed in awe at the sticky webs that clung to her fingers as she pulled them from her hair. "You've shot Lord Maltby. Poor sod," she said, staring through red puffy eyes at the injured man on the floor.

"*I'm* Nigel Maltby," Nigel said with a touch of pride. "The injured man is Paul Hampton, the man who murdered Professor Quayle. So there you have it. Now you know the truth."

"I don't want to know the truth," she spat with her mouth pulled down at the corners as though the words were poison and she had all she wanted of the unpleasant situation. "I don't ever want to know anymore about it. Please, you won't tell John what trouble I've gotten myself into?"

"Of course not. It's a little secret we can all keep to ourselves," Nigel said, winking at Julia in a flirtatious way that said, "expect to see more of me later."

165

"Thank you," Mae said, her face finally breaking into a trembling smile. "My, but you do have a beautiful castle."

Her serious tone sent them all into fits of laughter.

Chapter 28

Nigel and Julia walked silently together through the great rooms of the keep, one flowing graciously into another, a testament to the survival of the proud Maltby family. They went straight to Julia's room and plopped into the Chippendale wing chairs in front of the fireplace where they surveyed each other moodily while a busy servant coaxed the fire to life.

Julia was still numbed by how close they came to losing their lives. She was terribly grateful to Inspector Walpole for saving them. He obviously was not fooled by the photographs as thoroughly as she thought. She hoped above all that Rachel and Jeremy would leave their medieval retreat and go their separate ways without ever having to know the truth.

Her mind reran what Walpole said about Hampton's habit of showing up after the fact. Why hadn't she seen it? He convincingly stalked in late in a huff to see about the prowler at Dunrose Manor. His voice was a chilled echo through her body as she relived his grand entrance during the episode in the hall near the cello. Her father would have applauded his acting skills.

Now that she sat quietly thinking of it, there was something else in his approach in the hall that she did not recognize until now. There was the faint tink of metallic-ringed tassels bouncing on the top of stylish loafers. It was the same tink she heard below stairs the night of the murder. She jerked at the thought and felt a cold wave of goose bumps prickle her skin as if she were doused with a bucket of ice water. She pulled her chair closer to the struggling fire.

"I'm sorry, so sorry for placing your life in danger," Nigel said. "I can never forgive myself. Poor Rachel and Jeremy. What can I do to make it right with them? Perhaps I could refund their money. Would that suffice?"

"Oh, please, Nigel, don't talk about money at a time like this. I can't bear it. We were all fooled by Hampton."

"You're not going to leave tomorrow as planned, are you, Julia?" he asked. Mellow pensive eyes rested on hers and refused to let them go. "There are so many things we haven't had a chance to do. There's the jewelry, and the rest of the castle to explore...and you haven't even had a full tour of your future home, Dunrose Manor. It's quite a majestic house, you know, and it needs the love of a beautiful woman to make it complete. There is no question that that's where you belong."

Julia was transfixed by his speech. "So that's why you gave me the cello. You were planning to keep me here so we can both play it. I must say, I can't understand why you keep it in that dark back hall. I'm not sure I could ever bear to walk near it again."

"I don't know why the cello was placed in that spot originally. I once asked Grandfather about it, but he said he didn't know, that it had been there since he was born. You must understand that things are not moved about much in a place like Gorlachen. One must not risk breaking historical continuity."

Julia smiled at his devotion.

"All well and good, but you can use some help along that line." She picked up the tier of steps perched against the high bed and turned it over. The mark said, 'Made in Philadelphia.' "Not even English."

He laughed nervously. "A lot of things in the castle aren't English. There are priceless French, Italian, Spanish, and Oriental pieces. Maybe we can add some more American things to it--like yourself, for instance."

Was he offering marriage? Her breath caught at the thought. Why was she surprised? She was deeply attracted to him before she discovered he was her cousin. Then, abruptly, a black ponytail bobbed before her eyes.

"What about Annalisa?"

"Annalisa Bowers lives in a grand old manor house over that-a-way," he said and pointed to the west. "Our parents were friends and we played together occasionally when we were children. Later we had a date now and then. She came this week only to help me look like a tourist traveling with his girl. She went home every night, I swear it. she will be married this fall to a very wealthy Englishman.

There was nothing about Nigel that even remotely smacked of a tourist, Julia thought, looking him over carefully. His whole physical presence reeked of an English country gentleman filled to capacity with the rich heritage of his castle and the family title that goes with it. Was there a place for her in all of this?

"Will you stay, Julia? I beg you to stay."

"I...I don't know what to say. I'm so very American." She planned to go home to her tiny apartment tomorrow to pick up an uncertain life in New York City where she left off before coming here. All of hers and her parents' belongings were there. How could she make long-range promises on such short notice? She looked around the immense cold high-roofed bedroom and blew on her hands. "I mean...I require heat."

"I'm happy to report that Dunrose Manor is equipped with central heating." He laughed with delight. "And yes, I'd say you're very American. You have beautiful skin and teeth and a very interesting petite figure, but those clear blue-grey eyes sparkle with a lusty desire to be a Maltby to the limit. Now how could you accomplish it more perfectly? Come with me." He crossed the space between them and grasped her hand.

At the touch of his warm steady grip, Julia knew she would not leave Gorlachen tomorrow.

169

Chapter 29

Nigel collected Julia from her room at eight. They made a grand entrance into a dining room vibrating with gaiety as the relieved guests mingled to share their last evening together at Castle Gorlachen. Even Inspector Walpole popped in at the last minute to share in the fun.

The long candlelit table shimmered with a dazzling display of china and silver. Mauve, pink, and white roses from the gardens at Dunrose Manor were arranged in priceless Oriental vases and placed with the greatest care on marble columns throughout the room, their fragile scent magnified by waves of heat from the ancient fireplace.

What a way to live. Julia sipped a glass of claret while she marveled at the elegant surroundings. Could she ever be a part of this magnificence? She was certainly willing to try.

Abruptly she realized something was missing. She gazed over the bustling crowd. It was Paul Hampton. She and Nigel were so busy enjoying each other that, until this very moment, she failed to give Paul Hampton another thought. She missed him, she realized, missed the frank appraising eyes that seemed to glow like fireplace coals in any available light. She missed the often ludicrous and uncertain attempts of a working-class man to step into the shoes of an English lord. She was sorry it came to such a miserable end. He was cornered by the existence of the film, driven to terror and a passionate attempt at self-survival. Whatever motives caused him to set up the betrayal in the first place must have been out of character. Secretly she hoped the courts might, somehow, go easy on him. But how could they? And what was she thinking anyway? Didn't he try to kill her? She returned Nigel's covetous gaze from across the room and forced her thoughts back to the party. This was one evening she could enjoy without fear.

The guests suffered through an ill-conceived medieval play in the courtyard early in the afternoon, but the servants made up for it later with an unusually extravagant high tea. With the murder solved they were in a mood to join in an unforgettable festive evening in a fairy tale castle.

Julia and Nigel spent the afternoon exploring Dunrose Manor. With relaxed confidence, Julia watched proudly while Nigel took his rightful place at the head of the table after seating her at the other end. He took great care not to muss the full-skirted, silver brocade gown she wore that belonged to her grandmother. Julia found the Victorian dress that afternoon in the trunk room at Dunrose Manor. She simply could not resist wearing it. Nigel laughed fondly at her choice and subtly suggested she would tire soon enough at playing queen. Of course she would, but she intended to enjoy it to the fullest this evening.

That Dunrose Manor exceeded her expectations was an understatement. There was little about the house she would need to change. A good cleaning of the rooms and furniture, the replacement of a few broken or misplaced light fixtures, and the repair of tattered fabrics in draperies, bed hangings and stuffed furniture would restore it perfectly.

It was not often that Lord Maltby was in the mood for this evening's elegant expansive spending spree. The servants took the opportunity to put on the most extravagant performance of their careers. They served his favorite, a saddle of roast lamb with mint sauce, crusty roasted potatoes, and a myriad of colorful and savory vegetable dishes. A luscious cherry gateau with decorative ringlets of whipped cream ended the meal in a most satisfactory manner. In the bed and breakfast business servants knew that well-fed guests went away happy no matter what else befell them during their stay.

When the time was right, Julia listened with attention when Nigel stood up and tapped his crystal water goblet lightly with a silver spoon. The tink rang merrily through the room.

"My friends and guests of Gorlachen," he said, "I feel an explanation is due you, and I shall make it brief. You all know my true identity by now and the gist of what has taken place at Gorlachen these last few days. I must say, in my wildest imagination I don't believe I could have provided a more fitting backdrop for your medieval vacation."

The guests applauded with approval.

"Through a series of lies and deception, Paul Hampton gained my confidence and friendship to work his way into my home. As it turned out, he was not a trustworthy person and is charged with the murder of Professor Quayle and an attempt on the life of my dear cousin, Julia Maltby."

"Why, the blackguard," John Eldred said, his tongue fuzzy from too much drink. "He's probably the one who tried to rape my gorgeous wife."

The guests laughed and applauded with pure delight.

Mae, dressed in a bright red silk gown with a white crushed satin sash, beamed happily for the first time since her arrival at Gorlachen. She didn't bat an eye as she, Nigel, and Julia exchanged secretive glances. The three were quite fond of each other after their experiences over the last five days.

"We'll skip the details except to say that we owe a great debt to Inspector Walpole for his part in subduing Hampton," Nigel continued. He picked up his wine glass and extended it to the Inspector. "Cheers!"

"Cheers!" the group repeated lustily while Walpole rose and took a rather clumsy bow on his own behalf.

With dinner over, the guests milled around the room, each with his own version of how Walpole shot Hampton. They were reluctant to say good night after such a lovely evening. Friendships were cultivated that would not be easily forgotten. Individually they wished each other well as they prepared to go their separate ways early the next morning with promises to write, and a suggested possibility of all coming together again at the same time next year.

Julia's heart gave a lurch as she watched Rachel entangled in a goodbye hug with Jeremy and Sara. Rachel lost out on winning Jeremy. It was probably for the best, Julia decided, and it appeared that Sara had overcome her jealous dislike for Rachel. Perhaps it paved the way for the three to see each other in the States. Julia was pleased it turned out that way for them, but when would *she* see Rachel again?

Rachel disentangled herself and strolled over to Julia. Julia watched her dark eyes sweep over the brocade dress.

"You're not going home with me tomorrow, are you?"

Julia searched for the right words. "I...I can't, Rachel. I've discovered something elemental in my life--something I can't deny."

"I know, hon," Rachel said lightly. "Being a Maltby means more than I ever imagined." She took Julia's right hand in hers and gazed at the newly-acquired ring she wore. "Well now. I finally have a chance to do what I came here to do, but it's on the wrong hand, isn't it?"

"Give us some time," Julia said, blushing as happily and self-consciously as a school girl.

"Well, let's see." Rachel studied the stones from all angles with exaggerated gestures. "An approximate three-carat teardrop-cut diamond with fine clarity and color, surrounded by what appear to be perfectly matched flawless sapphires. The mounting is definitely antique eighteen-carat gold filigree." She looked up at Julia and smiled warmly. "I couldn't have chosen better myself."

They hugged and both looked away as tears blurred their vision.

"I'll miss you, Julia, but I'm ready now to go home and get to work. Maybe someday I'll meet a Prince Charming, preferably an English Lord with a lot of money?" They laughed together like old times.

Julia vowed then and there that she would never tell Rachel about the plot to implicate the various guests, including Rachel herself, in theft and murder at Castle Gorlachen. Never.

CPSIA information can be obtained at www.ICGtesting.com
Printed in the USA
268217BV00001B/85/P